W9-BUO-938

ALSO BY PHILIP R. CRAIG

A FATAL
VINEYARD
SEASON

A Martha's Vineyard Mystery

PHILIP R. CRAIG

SCRIBNER

SCRIBNER
1230 Avenue of the Americas
New York, NY 10020

Copyright © 1999 by Philip R. Craig

Text set in Baskerville

Manufactured in the United States of America

1   3   5   7   9   10   8   6   4   2

Library of Congress Cataloging-in-Publication Data
Craig, Philip R., 1933–
A fatal vineyard season: a Martha's Vineyard mystery/Philip R. Craig.
p. cm.
I. Title.
PS3553.R23F38   1999
813' .54—dc21   98–54710   CIP

ISBN 0-684-85544-5

For my daughter Kimberlie,
who lives in the faraway mountains
of Colorado,
but keeps part of her heart
on Martha's Vineyard

A FATAL VINEYARD SEASON

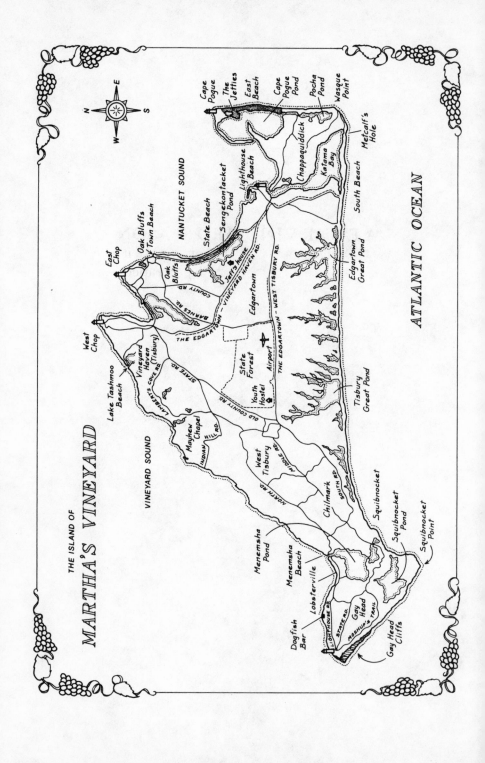

. . . The seed of wisdom did I sow
And with mine own hand wrought to make it grow;
And this was all the harvest that I reaped—
I came like water, and like wind I go.
—The Rubáiyát of Omar Khayyám

1

We had spent the night anchored up at the far end of Lagoon Pond and were heading back down toward the drawbridge at midmorning when I saw the big, black-hulled powerboat coming fast toward us, throwing a wide wake toward both sides of the pond. I don't like speeding powerboats, and I particularly don't like them when they're speeding at me. We were ghosting along in front of a small following wind and were in no shape to get out of anybody's way, so it was a relief to me when the boat curved off to our right and pulled smoothly alongside a dock on the Oak Bluffs side of the Lagoon. Beside the dock was a boathouse, and behind that was an embankment that was topped by a big, new house.

As the boat swept toward shore, I saw the swordfishing pulpit on her bow and then the name on her stern: *Invictus*. A moment later we were rocked by her wake, and Zee and I hung on to the kids until the waters quieted, making unkind comments about people who drove their boats the way the skipper of the *Invictus* drove his.

"You and your sister won't ever sail a boat like that, will you, Joshua?" Zee, holding Diana the huntress, who was hungry as always, looked at her firstborn, who was hooked in one of my arms while I held the tiller with my other.

Joshua shook his head. "No, Mom."

"Joshua isn't going to race stinkpots," I said. "He'll be a sailor, like his father. Won't you, Josh?"

Joshua, quick to catch on to parental biases, nodded. "Yes, Pa."

"Nice-looking boat, though," I said, looking at the *Invictus* as her skipper made her fast to the dock. She was a yacht, but with several features more typical of a fishing boat.

"I like a pulpit and a trawler hull," agreed Zee. "Too bad the guy doesn't know enough to keep his wake down when he comes in from outside."

We sailed slowly on toward the drawbridge under a fine fall sky. Labor Day was behind us, Martha's Vineyard was pretty much emptied of its summer people and its summer yachts, and Zee and I were on the last leg of an experimental test cruise to see how well we'd hold up with two little kids on board. We were amateur parents who had just begun to think we might survive Joshua when Diana the huntress had made her appearance, and we were right back at the starting line again. Still, it had seemed to us that the *Shirley J.* would be a good boat for kids; being beamy, she offered a good deal of room for her size, and because of the jiffy reefing system I'd installed, she was pretty easy to keep flat even in a breeze. Besides, catboats were pretty rough-and-ready vessels, and we didn't think the piles of gear that go with babies would do ours any harm.

And so we'd packed up and taken the little ones on their first cruise because you're never too young to go sailing and because Zee and I wanted to know if we were up to being a family afloat. We'd sailed from Edgartown to Hadley's the first day; then, the next day, we'd reached along the north shore of Naushon, had ducked through Robinson's Hole back into Vineyard Sound, and had pulled into Tarpaulin Cove for the night. Then we'd sailed back to Vineyard Haven, passed through the open drawbridge, and anchored far up in the Lagoon. And now we were headed home.

And we'd found out that we could, indeed, sail together, as long as we didn't mind tight quarters, for our little eighteen-foot Herreshoff, none too big for Zee and me even before we'd added Joshua and Diana to our household, was pretty stuffed with the essentials needed for children under two. One of the things that made the cruise possible was keeping some gear, and particularly the plastic bag full of used disposable diapers, in the dinghy we towed behind us. Without that dinghy, who knows what our feelings about family sailing might have been?

But we did have the dinghy and we were happy as we headed for home.

The drawbridge keeper opened his bridge for us, and we sailed into the outer Vineyard Haven harbor, then hooked to starboard, toward Nantucket Sound, rounded East Chop outside of the Oak Bluffs bluffs, and reached southeast, toward Edgartown.

As we passed the bluffs, I could see the big house that belonged to Stanley and Betsy Crandel up there at the top. It was one of the places I closed up in the fall, opened in the spring, and kept an eye on in the winter. I also took care of some boats, caught and sold fish, and did a little bit of a lot of things to supplement the small checks I got from Uncle Sam and the Boston PD as a consequence of having been blown up and shot while working for them earlier in my life. When I got home, I was scheduled to replace a leaky faucet at the Crandel house, in a bathroom off the kitchen, because a Crandel niece was coming in a few days for a short Vineyard holiday.

But that was later; this was now. Under light blue skies and over dark blue water, we headed down to Edgartown, tacked into the harbor, and made fast at our stake.

Zee buttoned her shirt and wiped Diana's mouth. "Home again, home again. Your girl child eats like a horse, Jefferson."

Like mother, like daughter. Zee, too, could eat like a horse and, much to the annoyance of her women friends, never gain an ounce. Moreover, it wasn't long after her babies were born that her belly was as flat as ever. It was quite unfair, said her friends. I thought it was just fine, but I doubted if Zee thought about it at all, any more than she thought about being beautiful.

I rowed us all ashore, then walked over to Manny Fonseca's woodworking shop and got the Land Cruiser, which I'd parked there so it wouldn't get a ticket from Edgartown's eagle-eyed parking police. Edgartown is getting so advanced in its thinking that it's no longer possible for a sailor or a fisherman to park on a side street and go to sea for a few days. You have to find some private place to put your car. I complain about it to the chief of police whenever I think of it, but a fat lot of good it does me.

"Good trip?" asked Manny.

"Finest kind."

"Timed it right," said Manny. "The one they call Elmer is down there in the Caribbean someplace. Wouldn't want to be out in a boat the size of yours if it comes this way."

"You won't get any argument from me. I don't want to be out in any size boat during a hurricane."

Hurricane Elmer had just been Tropical Depression Elmer when we'd left for our cruise, but the little portable radio we'd taken with us had informed us that he'd gotten bigger since.

I drove Zee and the little ones home, where they were welcomed by Oliver Underfoot and Velcro, the cats, who had been living alone while we'd been gone, but who hadn't suffered much because we'd left them plenty of food and water, and their little cat door had allowed them to get in and out of the house whenever they wanted. Then I went back to Collins Beach, where I ferried our traveling gear off the *Shirley J.*, tidied her up, put on the sail cover, filled out the log, and went ashore again.

Another successful sail, a successful sail being defined as one where you go out and come back again in one piece. It had, in fact, been more than just a successful sail. It had been a fine sail.

I climbed back into the truck and drove home.

Home. Where the heart is.

Zee had a vodka martini waiting. She put it in my hand. It was cold. "Ice," she said. "We haven't had any for a while." She touched her glass to mine and smiled her dazzling smile.

We sat on our balcony, holding a kidling apiece, and looked out onto the water we'd just sailed over. On the far side we could see the low line that was Cape Cod.

"Before the Derby starts, I've got to take these sprats over to visit with my folks," said Zee.

"And I've got to install a faucet at Betsy Crandel's place." I yawned. "So much to do, so little time. Sailing and visiting America and pursuing bluefish and bass. We lead a frenzied life."

Zee bounced Diana on her knee. "You can check out all our fishing gear while I'm gone so we'll be ready to hit the beach on opening day."

"I can do that," I agreed. The annual Martha's Vineyard Bass and Bluefish Derby was one of the East Coast's finest fishing tournaments, and we fished in it every year in hopes of one day getting the biggest fish. So far, it had never happened, but so what? This might be the year.

The evening light slanted from the west. We finished our drinks and went down for supper. Shrimp baked with sherry and garlic. What could be finer? I felt good. Later, glad to be in a double bed again, I slept wrapped in Zee's arms. On the morrow I'd go up to the Crandel place and install that faucet, little guessing how that mundane act would change my life.

2

The Crandel house is out on East Chop, on top of the Oak Bluffs bluffs. It's a big, rambling Victorian place, with weathered gray cedar shingles, a round tower on one corner, and broad verandas. From the front of the house you can look out over the Sound and see Cape Cod on the far side. It's a pretty snazzy place, all in all, and various Crandels have been summering there since the early twentieth century.

The current senior Crandels usually came down in May, when the Vermont snow was gone from the last ski slope, and usually headed elsewhere around mid-October. They were retired and seemed to split their time among New York City, Middlebury, and the Vineyard. They had a lot of kids and other kin, so the house was full of people all summer long. Or so it seemed when I happened to drive by between Memorial Day and Labor Day.

Perhaps having missed Auden's irony when he wrote of how each in his little bed conceived of islands where love was innocent, being far from cities, I had retired from combating the evils of the urban world and moved to Martha's Vineyard to live a peaceful life. By doing various odd bits of work, I managed to avoid taking a steady job, so I'd be able to go fishing whenever I wanted to, or take time out for dadding, which was a business I was still learning, just as Zee was still learning the momming game.

It had been no surprise to me that being a father would take some study and effort, but for some reason I'd always supposed that women just naturally knew how to be mothers. It was something in their genes or hormones, I'd thought; like their natural ability to keep house and tell when one color clashed with another.

Not so, I had discovered, as both Zee and I blundered our way through tyro parenthood, first with Joshua and then with his sister, Diana, the huntress, who sought food night and day.

"I thought you women were born knowing how to take care of kids," I'd once said to Zee, after both our darlings were temporarily asleep at the same time and we were lying in bed, a bit on the worn-out side. "I thought it was part of the great master plan, so us menfolk could go off hunting and fishing and know that everything was hunky-dory at home."

"Fah!" Zee had replied. "Don't be fooled by the Barbie dolls in frills that little girls play with. Personally, I think they should fit Barbie out with waders and a fly rod, so she can get rid of all those pink dresses and have some real fun with Ken. As for me, I wish I did know everything about children, but I don't." We were in the two-spoon position and she'd wriggled a bit closer. "That's why we have Dr. Spock."

If large families were a sign of expertise in child rearing, the Crandels were masters of the game. I'd gotten the housekeeping job for them through John Skye, because I took care of his island house and boat while he and Mattie and the twins were up in Weststock, where during the winter he professed about things medieval in the college there. He and Stanley Crandel went way back, to when both of them had been undergraduates, and when Crandel had mentioned a need for a guy to take care of his house, John had given him my name.

Stanley Crandel liked to claim that he was descended from John Saunders, the onetime Virginia slave who, in 1787, was, according to some, the first Methodist to preach on Martha's Vineyard. Stanley had a picture on his wall that was supposed to be of John, right beside a good photograph of a waterspout that had appeared out in Nantucket Sound in the late 1800s. Stanley's walls also held photographs of many, many Crandels and other family members in various poses, mostly taken in Oak Bluffs. The oldest of these pictures showed formally garbed Crandels looking a bit stiff in their very proper clothes, but the newer ones became increasingly informal. From beginning to end, they offered a pretty good pictorial history of twentieth-century Oak Bluffs society, especially that having to do with the lives and times of the well-to-do black bourgeoisie, who had been a major part of the town's public life for over a hundred years.

There were pictures of Crandels and kin at the Tabernacle during religious services (presumably Methodist?), Crandels eating ice cream at the beach, Crandels in boats, fishing or rowing or sailing, Crandels under the ancient oaks that gave the town its name, Crandels having picnics, young Crandels playing baseball while older Crandels watched, Crandels of all ages playing tennis, Crandels getting married, Crandel babies being displayed by their proud parents, and so forth. There were so many pictures that I wondered, when first I saw them, if maybe the Crandels were heavily invested in photography stock.

They were a good-looking bunch, for the most part, and came in various shades of light and dark, as is often the case when bloodlines are mixed, as most are. One consistent element in their faces was a look of intelligence. And if intelligence is linked to success and success can be defined in terms of wealth and professional repute, the Crandels had their share of it, since their numbers included doctors, lawyers, professors, a general or two, a young actress, and other such folk.

Of course not all Crandels and Crandel kin were totally virtuous and successful. There were, no doubt, failures of various kinds, and there was at least one famous, or infamous, criminal: Cousin Henry Bayles, the scandal of the otherwise very respectable Philadelphia Bayleses, who had worked his way to the top of his hometown's black mob before leaving the city just in front of angry gangster rivals and taking up quiet retirement in a small house in Oak Bluffs, well across town from the big Crandel mansion. Cousin Henry and his wife were actually in one of the photographs of a Crandel lawn party, but they were far in the background. As far as I could tell, Cousin Henry and the Stanley Crandels didn't do any significant socializing.

I had been working for the Crandels for five years when the first killing involving them occurred. Actually, the Crandels were only indirectly linked to the death, but since they weren't the sort of people who were mixed up in such things, a lot of people were surprised and shocked by the news, or so they said. In any case, the circumstances of that death and the other later ones were the subject of considerable conversation by both Crandels and non-Crandels.

Of course killings take place in the best of families, although admittedly they happen more often among the dumb, the illiterate, the drunks and drug users, the down-and-outers, life's losers, the people "known," as they say, to the police, to the courts, to the social services people, and to the emergency wards. It is sad but true that people who live on the rough edges of society are those most susceptible to violence. Most of it is done by them and to them, and they can't seem to help themselves. Jesus said the poor will always be among us; so, too, will life's losers.

But not all killings involve them. Some involve people like the Crandels. And me.

When I'd opened the Crandel house the previous spring, I'd doubted if an ancient faucet in a little bathroom off the Crandel kitchen would last the summer and had so told Betsy Crandel, the matriarch of the clan, when she'd called me in May to tell me when they'd be getting down to the island.

Ever cozy with a dollar, which might partially explain

why the Crandels had so many of them, she had said they'd see how long it would last. And, in fact, it had lasted all summer. But in early September, a couple of weeks before the Derby was scheduled to begin, I got another call from Betsy Crandel.

She told me that the faucet was definitely on its last legs and had to be replaced, that she and Stanley were going to Switzerland for the rest of the fall and wouldn't be back on the Vineyard until spring, but that their niece Julia and her friend Ivy Holiday would be arriving in a week or so and would be using the house for a while, after which I could close it up for the winter.

Ivy Holiday, eh? That was interesting. Julia Crandel, I recalled, was the current actress in the family.

"I'll order another faucet," I said, "but it'll take a few days to get here."

"That's fine, J.W.," said Betsy. "When it comes in, you just install it. I'll tell the girls you're coming, so they'll be expecting you. How was your summer?"

"We've been trying to learn how to be parents to two kids instead of just one, and so far we're finding out that it's a lot different."

"That's wonderful! There is nothing like a family!"

Women are quite capable of discussing and watching children for hours at a time. Betsy was no exception, so I changed the subject before she got going on the joys and tribulations of her decades of parenting.

"I think Zee met Ivy Holiday when she was out in California. Isn't Ivy the one who caused such a stir at the Academy Awards ceremony?"

"Oh, you saw that, did you? Some people were scandalized!" Betsy herself sounded more amused than scandalized.

Actually, I hadn't seen the show, but it had been greatly commented upon in the papers for the next several days, and Zee had followed the stories with interest.

"I read about it," I said.

"Taking off her blouse like that," said Betsy with a laugh. "My, my! She's certainly political!"

The scandal was that Ivy Holiday, who had just handed out the Best Supporting Actress award, had then taken control of the microphone to rage against the exploitation of women as sex objects in films and, to make her argument more dramatic, had shed her upper garments in front of a TV audience of millions before walking bare breasted off the stage, chin held high.

A lot of humor and pious talk about moral standards had resulted from Ivy's performance, but not much had changed with regard to moviemakers treating women as sex objects. My own response had been mild interest in the question of just how Ivy's bared bosom was intended to serve as a repudiation of the exploitation of women in films. But then I never did have much of a grasp of symbolism.

Anyway, Ivy was now coming to the Vineyard. Zee would be pleased to hear it. She and Ivy had met and apparently hit it off well during Zee's brief visit to Hollywood as an actress.

The precise extent of Zee's own time on the silver screen was supposed to be soon revealed to us because *Island of Emeralds*, the movie that had been partially filmed on the Vineyard, and in which Zee had a whole line of dialogue, was going to have its premiere, or one of them, at least, on the island. Since Zee was the movie's most notable local extra, and I was her husband, we had been invited to the opening, at which time we would discover how much of Zee's face was now on the cutting-room floor.

Which gave me a thought. "Is Ivy here for the big premiere?" I asked.

There was a short pause before Betsy answered, "I don't know if she'll be down that long. I think she just wanted to get away from L.A. for a while. She and Julia have gotten pretty close over the past few months, so Julia invited her here for a vacation."

Julia, I knew, had already been an actress in New York,

but had gone west in hopes of making it in the movies. She was certainly pretty enough, as her photographs attested, and if that plus the Crandel brains was what it took to get her onto the screen, she was a shoo-in. However, I had read that brains had little to do with a successful film career, and that looks weren't everything, either. Apparently it was some sort of special something that made you a star, and beauty and brains played second fiddle to that, whatever it was.

And whatever it was, some people thought Zee had it. Which was why she had been spotted by the moviemakers on the Vineyard and had been talked into taking her one-line role in *Island of Emeralds*.

Life is like that sometimes: them that wants, don't get, and them that don't, do.

"How's Julia's career coming along?" I asked.

"I guess she's gotten some advertising jobs on TV. Her mother says that she was a dancing mop who cleaned a kitchen like magic, or something like that. And that she keeps standing in the meat lines or whatever they call those things where people try out for roles. She's not the type to give up easily, but she's pretty tight-lipped about her life out there. I wish I was going to be here when she arrives. I'd sit her down and get all of the dope straight from her. Then I could tell her mother what she's been up to. Some daughters tell everyone else before they tell their mothers. Julia's one of them." Betsy laughed.

"I'll tell Zee that Ivy's coming down," I said. "Maybe the two of them can get together."

"That would be nice for both of them. See you in the spring. Have a good winter."

Betsy rang off and presumably headed for Switzerland.

3

The faucet got to Martha's Vineyard the same day that Ivy Holiday and Julia Crandel did, so it happened that I was in the little bathroom off the Crandel kitchen when they arrived at the house. I heard a feminine voice from the living room, calling, "Hello? Hello? Is anybody there? Is that you, Mr. Jackson? Hello?"

There was an odd note in the voice, I thought. It was Julia's voice, I was sure, because my name had been used, and Betsy Crandel had said she'd tell Julia that I might come by to install the faucet. But what accounted for that note of . . . what? . . . fear? . . . caution at least . . . in her voice, as though she thought someone else besides me might be there?

"I'm in here," I called. "I'm putting in this faucet."

Cautious footsteps came across the wide pine-board floors of the living room toward the kitchen. At the kitchen door, the voice came again: "Hello? Mr. Jackson?"

I deliberately dropped a wrench on the floor before standing and going to the bathroom door. I looked across the kitchen at the two young women and put a smile on my face. It wasn't hard. They were real beauties, still dressed in the California mode.

"Hi." I pointed a finger. "You're Julia. You look like a Crandel." I reaimed the finger. "And that makes you Ivy. Welcome to the Vineyard. I'm J. W. Jackson."

"Oh," said Julia, her hand near her throat. "It is you, Mr. Jackson. Aunt Betsy said you might be doing some work here." She let her hand fall and put on a smile. "It's so nice to meet you."

"Call me J.W." I poked a thumb over my shoulder. "I should be here about another fifteen minutes, then the place is all yours. I just opened some of the upstairs bedroom windows to let in some air."

"Thank you." She paused. "Are you all alone here?"

"All alone. Nobody else has been here since Stan and Betsy left for the winter."

The two of them looked at each other. "Well, then," said Julia, "I guess we'll bring in our things."

"Nice to meet you, Mr. Jackson," said Ivy Holiday. Her eyes flicked over me, and she flashed a quick Hollywood smile.

"Call me J.W. Nice to meet the two of you, too."

I went back to the faucet and finished installing it. When I came out into the kitchen, I could hear the women in the living room. I went there and found them with their luggage. "All done," I said. "Enjoy yourselves."

They exchanged quick glances. "Wait a moment," said Julia. "I know this is going to seem silly, but would you mind showing us around the house? Ivy's never been here, and it's been a long time since I was. Would you mind?"

I put my toolbox by the front door. "No, I don't mind at all."

I had been through all of the house many times during the previous five years, and I made sure that I showed them every room. And every closet, all of which I opened. And the attic. And the basement. And the three-car garage. I showed them the locked doors and windows on the lower floor, and the windows I'd opened upstairs that morning.

When we were back in the living room, Julia seemed happier.

"Thank you very much," she said.

"I'm in the book," I said. "If you need anything, just give me a call."

"Thank you."

I looked at Ivy. "My wife may be calling you."

She tilted her head to one side. "Your wife?"

"Zee Jackson. You met in Hollywood last year, when she was out there shooting a scene in *Island of Emeralds*. She heard you were coming to the island and said she'd like to get together with you. She's going to the mainland tomorrow, but maybe you can fit each other into your schedules."

Ivy's dark brows lifted. "Ah, Zee. You're her husband. Well, I must admit that it never crossed my mind that the Zee Jackson I met out there would be married to the J. W. Jackson I just met today." She put out her hand and took mine. "How do you do?"

Her hand was warm and firm and lingering. "There are a lot of Jacksons in this world," I said. "Too many, some might say. There's no reason you'd tie Zee to me."

"Well, tell Zee that I want to see her. Tell her to call me and that if I don't hear from her, I'll call her."

"I'll do that." I got my hand back and picked up my toolbox. I looked at Julia Crandel. "To repeat myself, if you need anything, let me know. I can be here in fifteen minutes. It might be a good idea to keep the downstairs doors and windows locked, just in case some drunk forgets where he lives and tries to get into your house by mistake."

Julia nodded. "Thank you. We will. Come on, Ivy. You can have the big room I usually use, because you're the guest of honor. I'll sleep next door." I thought the lightness in her voice seemed feigned.

I went out and drove home, wondering why she was so nervous, and whom they didn't want to meet. I thought of stopping by the Oak Bluffs PD and asking the guys to keep an eye on the women, but on second thought realized I didn't really have any reason to ask them to do that. Besides, two women who looked as good as Julia Crandel and Ivy Holiday would soon be under police observation anyway, along with observation by most other males who saw them.

If I were still single, I'd have joined the observers, in fact, but I was a married man who had two women at home who took up all of my girl-watching time.

I did think a bit of Ivy, though. The Ivy I'd seen, slender and a bit of a flirt, didn't look like the Ivy I'd read about, the one who'd bared her bosom to the world and pontificated against pornography. But as the jazzman said, one never knows, do one?

At home, the other members of my family were out in the yard, sopping up some September sunshine.

"Ivy wants you to get in touch," I said to Zee, taking Diana the huntress out of her arms. "She says if you don't call her, she'll call you."

"Oh, good. How long is she going to be on the island?"

That I did not know, but I did know that she was probably in the Crandel house even as we spoke.

"I'll call her right away," said Zee. "You are the kid herder for the nonce."

"Does that make me a kidboy?" I asked Diana. "Do I get to wear a big hat and spurs?"

Diana drooled at me, and Zee rolled her eyes and went into the house, as Joshua, who was still a bit jealous of his sister, came across the yard to claim a share of my attention.

"Well, Josh," I said, "do you know yet when your mom's movie is going to be shown here?"

Joshua didn't know any more about it than I did. I knew it was going to be shown later in the year, but no one local seemed to know quite when.

"Are the stars going to be there to dazzle the crowd?" I asked.

Josh thought they might be. More important, he thought he should be up on my chest where Diana was. It seemed like a reasonable request, so I shifted Diana to one arm and picked him up with the other. We strolled around the yard, admiring the remaining flowers in their boxes and hanging pots, and the remains of the vegetables in the raised beds.

Zee came out of the house and lay down on the as-good-as-new lounge we'd gotten for a pittance at a yard sale. "I've invited them down for cocktails tonight," she said, stretching and yawning. "Meanwhile, I think I'll take a nap. Wake me up when they get here."

They weren't going to get here for several hours, but Zee had had both kids all morning and deserved a break, so she could nap if she wanted to. I looked at her lying there in her shorts and old blue shirt. With her sleek body and blue-black hair, she reminded me, as she often did, of a jungle cat, a dark leopard. Even her deep, dark eyes sometimes had a feral quality to them, especially since the births of her children. It was the look of a lioness, a creature whose cubs you'd best leave alone.

"You snooze," I said. "I will take the offspring for a ride."

"I'll come, too!" She jumped up.

"I thought you were going to take a nap."

"Later. Ride first, nap second. The best of all possible worlds. Where do you plan to go?"

"I plan to go to Oak Bluffs and let my children ride the Flying Horses. I figure on standing in the middle and holding a kid on a horse on each side. You're never too young to ride the Flying Horses."

"Or too old!" said Zee.

True. The Flying Horses in Oak Bluffs are said to be the oldest continually operating carousel in the United States. I've often wondered if there are other carousels making the same claim. Maybe there are Oldest Continually Operating Carousels in lots of places, just like, I'm told, there are dozens of England's Oldest Pubs in Britain. In any case, the Flying Horses are old enough, and Joshua and Diana were old enough to ride them if they wanted to.

"Tell me about Ivy Holiday," I said to Zee as we drove.

"What do you want to know?"

"Well, you don't need to tell me she's beautiful, because

I've seen her in person, and you don't need to tell me she took off her shirt at the Academy Awards, and you don't need to tell me that she's controversial and political, because I've read about her since her striptease. You can maybe start by telling me what kind of an actress she is."

"She's a good actress. And she's beginning to get good parts. A lot of people think she'd make it big faster if she'd keep her mouth shut about politics, but she won't. And of course she's a woman and she's black, and that makes things even harder. There aren't many good roles for women out in Hollywood, and there are even fewer for a black woman."

I'd been wondering about the open-mouth part of Ivy's reputation. "Does she have enemies out there? People who'd just as soon she got run over by a truck?"

Zee frowned and nodded irritably. "Of course she has enemies. You can't be famous and not have enemies. She has enemies who envy her success, and enemies who hate her because of her politics, and enemies who hate her because of the color of her skin. There are racists and haters everywhere, and because she's famous, she has more than her share mad at her."

"Is there anybody in particular who might be giving her trouble?"

Zee looked at me. "What do you mean? Why do you ask?"

I told her what I'd observed at the Crandel house. "Julia seemed especially spooky," I said. "They were both a little nervous when they came in, and Julia didn't begin to settle down until I went through the whole house with them and showed them that no one else was there."

"Maybe they were just being careful. Women have to be that way."

"Maybe."

"Most men don't understand how cautious women have to be. If I were a young woman alone in a big, empty house,

I'd probably be nervous, too. You're a man and you're big, so you don't know what it's like."

I had a hard time imagining Zee being afraid to be alone, especially in light of the little row of trophies on the fireplace mantel that attested to her abilities with the customized .45 she used at pistol competitions.

"The point is," I said, "that they didn't seem to be nervous in that normal sort of way. They didn't kid about it, for instance. Julia especially was serious. And it didn't seem to be a generalized sort of worry about being alone; it seemed pretty specific. As though they had some reason to be nervous."

Zee sat silent for a while. Then she said, "Well, maybe the stalker got out of jail. Or maybe they were afraid there might be another stalker they didn't know about."

"Stalker? What stalker?"

Stalkers were everywhere, and they were bad business. They were men, mostly, and their victims were mostly women, often women with restraining orders against the stalkers. Ex-wives, wives, girlfriends, and women who were none of these and didn't want to be. Occasionally the stalker was a woman with a vendetta. And the thing that made stalkers so dangerous was that they often didn't care if they got caught. They wanted to possess or control their victims, and if they couldn't possess or control them, they wanted them dead, and often they killed themselves after killing their victims. Theirs was one of the many forms of love that makes human beings so inexplicably profane.

"There was a stalker after Ivy," said Zee. "Two years ago. Maybe you read about it. A young guy named Mackenzie Reed who decided she was the woman for him and went after her. You were a cop; you know how it goes. He wrote hundreds of letters to her; he got her unlisted telephone number; he found out where she lived; he knocked on her door; he stood across the street waiting for her to come out so he could accost her; he followed her. She got restraining orders, and she changed her phone number, and finally she moved in with another young actress named Dawn Dawson. She did everything she could, but he didn't go away, and one day when Ivy was away from the apartment, he slaughtered Dawn Dawson with a knife. Do you remember that?"

I don't pay much attention to faraway crimes. One reason I'd moved to Martha's Vineyard was so that I didn't have to deal with crime at all. Of course I'd rapidly learned that you can't escape the world by moving to an island. But I was still trying.

"I remember something about it," I said. "The guy said he didn't do it, but the jury said he did and put him away. I can't imagine that he's out this soon, even with the loony justice system we have these days."

"Well, maybe the system is loonier than you think. Maybe he is out, and maybe Ivy and Julia know it."

Maybe. Maybe they didn't even have prisons in California anymore. Maybe prisons were politically incorrect in California. Maybe they let their stalkers and murderers walk free after a couple of weeks of counseling. In California all things are possible. What others call madness, Californians call the norm.

I took a right off Circuit Avenue and a left onto Kennebec and found a parking place on Ocean, on the park, a couple of blocks from the Flying Horses. We got the little ones out of the car and headed for the carousel.

As we walked, I wondered why Julia seemed more nervous than Ivy. Did she know something Ivy didn't know? Or did Ivy know something Julia didn't know? Or was Julia the one with an enemy? Or was I imagining the whole thing?

"Look, Pa," said Joshua, pointing. "Flying Horses."

And he was right. We were there. So in we went, leaving Ivy, Julia, and their problems behind.

— 4 —

Joshua was tired and Diana was hungry (what else?) when we got home. We split the kid-changing and -feeding jobs and were surprised when both of our offspring actually went to sleep at the same time.

"Well," said Zee as we stood in the living room listening to the unusual afternoon silence, "this is a rare moment. What should we do with it?"

It was probably going to be the last of its kind before she got back from her visit to America. "I have an idea," I said, running a finger down her neck and across her shoulder.

She put her arms up around my neck. "I like living with you," she said. "Half the time you're totally predictable and the other half you aren't. It's a nice imbalance."

"Which half is this?"

"The predictable half. Come on!"

We headed for the bedroom.

"The first step in that being fruitful and multiplying command has something to be said for it," said Zee afterward as we washed each other off in the outdoor shower. "Maybe I'll just ship the kids to Mom, and I'll stay here with you."

"With both of them gone, we could probably multiply beyond all measure, if we tried," I said.

More than one young parent has remarked that after you have one child it's often hard to find an uninterrupted moment to have another. The Jackson plan had been to have two, preferably one of each gender, which we had managed, or maybe three just in case we happened, sometime or other, to be more passionate than prudent, which, with us, was always a possibility.

However, Zee's Genesis reference notwithstanding, she and I were now back in the Chaucerian mode of lovemaking, holding, as did old Geoffrey, that it was more for delyte than world to multiply.

I scrubbed her back and washed her long blue-black hair, and then, while the small fry still slept, the two of us lay out on our lawn chairs and perfected our all-over tans in the thin light of the westing sun. Oliver Underfoot and Velcro, the two cats, joined us and lay in the shade of the lounges.

I wished Zee and the little ones weren't going away, but I didn't plan to go with them. Maria, Zee's mother, was a bit too religious for my tastes, and still, I suspected, wished that Zee had stayed married to her first husband, the doctor, instead of ending up with me. This even though Paul Madieras, M.D., known to me as Paul the Jerk, had gotten the hots for another woman after nurse Zee had worked long to help put him through medical school. I had never actually met Paul the Jerk, but anyone who left Zee for another woman had to have something seriously wrong with him. Maria, however, still loved him because he was, after all, a doctor, and doctors, especially young, handsome Portuguese ones, were next to saints in her pantheon of the Good, the True, and the Beautiful.

Better, all in all, for me to stay at home and tend the gardens and cats.

Zee and I climbed into shorts and shirts and went to tend the tykes.

Julia and Ivy came down our long, sandy driveway a bit after five, as the evening was falling, and parked in our yard.

Ivy and Zee embraced like long-lost sisters, and Ivy introduced Zee and Julia to each other. Then, there being a cool September wind blowing in from the sound, we all went into the house, where the children and the cats were waiting.

After the visitors' obligatory and probably even sincere cooing and oohing over the kidlings, I offered drinks to all.

"Zee and I will be drinking vodka on the rocks with olives," I said, "but we have all sorts of other stuff, hard and soft, too. What would you like?"

The visitors would have white wine, just like the ladies, the good ones at least, always have in the soap operas. I played host and brought out smoked bluefish pâté, cheese, and crackers, along with the drinks. By the time I'd done that, the women were in seemingly happy conversation. I sat in my favorite chair and listened.

It reminded me of hearing a conversation in the Confessional. Not the one in the Catholic church; the one in the Fireside bar in Oak Bluffs. The owners of the Fireside, which was often crowded with both the high and the low life of the Vineyard, had recently added some booths against the back wall, and it was soon discovered that whoever was talking in the last booth in the row could be clearly heard in the booth next door. This inexplicable auditory phenomenon quickly gave the last booth its name: the Confessional. None of the regulars would sit there unless they wanted their conversation to be totally public, but strangers were never informed of the Confessional's peculiar auditory characteristic and sometimes gave the lucky occupants of the next booth, known sardonically as priests, very satisfactory entertainment.

I had been tipped off to this by Bonzo, who swept the Fireside's floors and cleaned its tables. Bonzo had once been a bright lad, I'd been told, but some bad acid had done him in years before I met him, and now he was only a gentle child.

"It's like in church, J.W.," he'd said in his wide-eyed way. "It's like you was the priest, you know? They talk and you listen. Sometimes the people listening even give them a penance, just like Father Joe does. I think it's sort of funny, but maybe it isn't. What do you think, J.W.?"

"I think I won't sit in the Confessional," I'd said.

Bonzo had nodded thoughtfully. "Yeah. Yeah, I think that might be a good idea, maybe. You're smart, J.W., you know that?"

Good old Bonzo.

Half listening now to the three women talking together made me wonder what real priests must hear in the pursuit of their spiritual duties as they listened to confessions. I doubted whether the most experienced of police officers were told more tales of the dark and quirky side of life than were priests.

I was glad I had gone into another trade.

I became aware that the women were talking about the stalker and began to listen.

"He can't be out of prison already," said Zee. "The man's a killer!"

"Oh, he's still in prison," said Julia. "He won't be out for a long time. But he still writes to Ivy! I don't know how he does it, but he does!"

"I give the letters to my lawyer whenever I get them," said Ivy. "He says there's no law against writing letters."

"It's maddening!" said Julia. "You can't imagine the things that man says. He wants to marry Ivy. And he tells her what they'll do afterward. It's obscene." Julia looked at Ivy. "I don't know how you even read them anymore. I'd just pass them on." She shivered.

"Mackenzie Reed's in prison," said Zee in her soothing nurse's voice. "He can't hurt anyone again."

Julia leaned forward. "But maybe it's not just him. I think he's got a friend who's not in jail. Who's outside!"

Zee gave her a sharp look. "Who?"

Julia and Ivy exchanged glances. "We don't know," said Ivy.

"But we know he's there," said Julia.

"How do you know?"

Julia's face was joyless. "Because somebody's mailing

those letters." She hesitated. "And because of what happened to Jane Freed and Dick Hawkins."

"Who are Jane Freed and Dick Hawkins? And what happened to them?"

"Jane was my therapist," said Ivy. "After Mackenzie Reed
killed Dawn, I needed one." Ivy looked quickly at Julia.
"She was Julia's therapist first, and Julia told me about her,
and I went to her. She was just what I needed. I could tell
her anything. Everything. It really helped."

As I listened, I remembered more about the case, which
had been greatly publicized because of its sensational ele-
ments: Hollywood, a stalker, a beautiful actress slain and
mutilated, and another lovely actress, the intended victim,
surviving by sheer chance. The story had irony, violence,
and sensation enough for anyone.

They'd nailed Mackenzie Reed, still bloody, coming out of
the apartment, inside of which Dawn Dawson's mutilated
body was still warm. At the trial, an overwhelming case pre-
sented by the prosecution had forced the defense to put Reed
on the stand. He'd admitted having phoned, written, and followed Ivy, and to loving her perhaps beyond measure. He'd
admitted that he had, indeed, been in the apartment, after
finding the door ajar, saying he'd gone inside because it was
his first chance to actually get into a place where she lived. But
he'd denied killing Dawn Dawson, saying he'd found her
already dead and had gotten bloody from touching her to see
if she were still alive. He said he'd tried to run away because
he knew he'd be blamed for her killing because of his obses-
sion with Ivy. He swore he was innocent of murder.

It had taken the jury only two hours to find him guilty,
and no one thought they'd rushed to judgment.

"What happened to Jane Freed?" asked Zee.

"She was killed about a year after Ivy started seeing her,"
said Julia. "They think some drug addict broke into her
office and that Jane found him there and he killed her. They
never found out who did it."

"How awful," said Zee.

Julia nodded. "For everyone. I guess Jane kept some medicines there, and this guy, whoever he was, was after them. He killed her with a paperweight she had there on her desk. They found her the next day."

I said, "Who's Dick Hawkins?"

"It's really unbelievable," said Ivy, looking at me. "Dick owns the apartment Julia and I have been sharing since . . . since Dawn was killed. He's not only been our landlord, he's been a good friend to us. A sort of father figure and protector. Then, last month, somebody stole Dick's car, and when Dick tried to stop him, the guy ran him down! Right there in front of our apartment building. He's still in the hospital and may never walk again."

"They found the car," said Julia, "but they never found the driver." She and Ivy both had large eyes as they looked at me. "It's as though everybody we know is getting killed. Everyone we get close to. I know it's silly to say this, but it's like we have the kiss of death. If we like you or love you, you die."

Ivy looked at me. "I know you were wondering why we wanted you to go around the house with us. We're being very careful."

"All that happened in California," I said, "and you're a long way from California right now. You're right to be careful, because we've got our share of wackos on the East Coast, but I don't think you're cursed with the fatal touch or anything like that, and I think that being three thousand miles from L.A. is probably good insulation against whatever happened out there."

"But two people are dead," said Ivy, studying me with those great dark eyes, "and another one almost died. Three of my friends. Three people who were close to me and tried to help me."

"It's a rotten world sometimes," I said. "But there's no pattern to the things that happened to your friends, so one thing probably had nothing to do with any other. It was just the fickle finger of fate. Sometimes a lot of bad things happen at about the same time for no reason at all, and we get caught up in the mess. I think that's what's happened to you. I think you should both forget this notion that you have the touch of death, or that your friends are doomed, and try to have a vacation. I think you both need one."

Julia sighed and sat back. "That's what we've been saying to ourselves. We know you're right, but . . ."

"No buts," said Zee in a matronly tone that impressed me because she was barely older than her two guests. "You put those terrible things behind you and relax. It's September and you're on Martha's Vineyard. September is the best time to be anywhere north of the equator, and the Vineyard is no exception to the rule. Most of the tourists are gone, the water is still warm, we only have one hurricane left and it's way down south, so all is well. You should put California out of your minds."

The two young women exchanged looks, then put smiles on their faces. "Yes," said Julia. "You're right. We'll just be vacationers like everybody else."

"We'd love to have you up for drinks before we go," said Julia later as they got into their car.

"Tomorrow I'm off with the kids to see my mama over in America," said Zee. "I'm afraid I won't be around for a while."

"Too bad," said Ivy. She looked at me. "Maybe you'll come by, J.W."

"I've been known to have a cocktail," I said.

The car drove away.

"She has great come-hither eyes, doesn't she?" said Zee.

"Who?"

"You know who."

"Oh, her."

Martha's Vineyard is a magic place that can isolate you from the real world for a while and cleanse your soul, and I

hoped that it would do that for Ivy Holiday and Julia Crandel. But as the old Indian medicine singer said when his
spell failed, sometimes the best magic doesn't work. Two
nights later, someone kicked in the front door of the Crandel house, took a knife from the kitchen, and went upstairs
after Ivy and Julia.

— 5 —

It happened the second evening after I had put Zee and the children on the *Schamonchi* and seen them off to New Bedford. I was home alone late that night, reading and feeling wide-awake and lonesome in our double bed, when the phone rang. It was Julia Crandel.

"Come quick! There's a man with a knife!"

"Call 911," I said, feeling cold and emotionless the way you sometimes do when there's a crisis. "I'm on my way. Are you both safe right now?"

"Yes! Yes! But hurry! Hurry!"

I got into shorts, Teva sandals, and a sweatshirt, then took Zee's little Beretta 84F out of the gun cabinet and slapped a magazine into it. It was less bulky than my old S and W police .38 and had more firepower to boot. Ten minutes later, after some illegal driving, I pulled up in front of the Crandel house.

There were lights in every window and police cruisers at the curb. It was just after midnight, but lights in neighboring houses were also going on, and people were beginning to come out onto their porches and into the street.

An Oak Bluffs police officer held up a hand as I walked across the lawn. "Sorry, sir. I'm afraid you'll have to go back to the street."

I gave him my name and told him about the call I'd gotten. He listened without changing expression, then pulled out his radio and spoke into it. After a moment, he nodded and put the radio back on his belt. "Okay, I guess you can go on in."

I went up onto the porch, where I met another police officer. We both went in through the front door. It was a heavy door in a solid frame, but the frame was splintered where the lock had been. There was also a bolt lock on the door, but it hadn't been shot home. If it had been, the door wouldn't have been kicked open so easily. If they'd been in New York or in Los Angeles or in any other city, Ivy and Julia would have used that bolt lock, but in Oak Bluffs, in spite of the stalker, they hadn't felt the need. I could understand that feeling since I usually don't lock the doors of our house even though I know perfectly well that percentage-wise there are probably just as many housebreakers and other bad guys on the island as anywhere else.

In the living room I found Lisa Goldman, the chief of the OBPD, a couple of other police officers, and Ivy and Julia. The latter two were seated on a couch close together, looking paler than when last we'd been together.

Seeing me, Julia jumped up and hugged my arm. "I'm glad you're here. I'm sorry I called you. But . . ." She paused and brushed at her forehead with her hand. "I'm not making much sense, am I?"

"You're making enough," I said. I looked over her head at Lisa Goldman. She and I had known each other for years, even though I'd never spent much time in OB, if you didn't count my mostly bachelor visits to the Fireside. "What happened?" I asked.

Lisa Goldman didn't look like a police chief. She had one of those faces that doesn't change much after junior high school. Although she was Zee's age, she still looked about fifteen years old. Her face had deceived many a perp, who mistook her for an innocent when she was anything but that, and her gentle manner gave no hint of her ability to handle herself in a scuffle quite nicely, thank you, if a scuffle was necessary. However, like most cops, Lisa preferred to talk hard cases into accepting arrest, and she was quite good at it. She was, in fact, a savvy, experienced cop who only happened to look like a schoolgirl.

Now, she poked a thumb toward the door. "Intruder kicked the door in. Went into the kitchen and got a knife, then went upstairs and tried to get into Miss Holiday's room. She'd locked her door when she'd gone to bed and was reading when she heard the noise downstairs. Then the guy came up and put the knife blade right through a panel in her bedroom door. There's a connecting door between her room and Miss Crandel's room, so she ran in there, and the two of them jammed chairs under the doorknobs of the two doors leading to the room and called us. Maybe the guy heard the sirens, or maybe he got spooked for some other reason, but after he gave Miss Holiday's door a couple of kicks and did a little carving on it with the knife, he split. We found the knife out on the lawn. It looks like it was wiped clean. That's about it."

"Any ideas about who it was?"

"Yeah," said a young cop. "We got an idea, but having an idea ain't enough to arrest anybody." He sounded angry.

"Who?" I asked Lisa.

She opened her mouth, but before she could speak, the young cop said, "Alexandro Vegas, that's who. The son of a bitch!"

"Now, Mickey," said Lisa in her soothing voice, "we don't know that. Don't jump to conclusions."

"Or if it wasn't Alexandro, it was his big brother, Alberto," said mad Mickey.

"That's enough, Mickey," said Lisa in a voice that was less soothing.

Mickey opened his mouth, but then shut it again. "Yes, ma'am."

Lisa said, "The guy cleaned the knife, but we'll dust things here and upstairs in case he touched something else. Of course there'll be dozens of prints and most of them will belong to one Crandel or another, but we might get lucky. The important thing is that these ladies kept their heads and did everything right, so nobody got hurt."

"But if scared was hurt, we'd both be in the emergency ward," said Julia in a shivery voice.

"The neighbors are all up anyway," said Lisa, "so we'll ask around and find out if anybody saw anything. Mickey, you and Howard and Jane go out and start talking to the people who are up and about."

"Yes, ma'am," said Mickey, who was probably glad to have a reason to leave his chief's presence. He went out the door.

"I'll have somebody come by in the morning and fix that door," said Lisa to Julia and Ivy. "Meanwhile, you can use the bolt to keep it shut."

"You aren't just going to go away, are you?" asked Julia. "What if he comes back?"

"I'll leave an officer outside," said Lisa.

Julia, who was still standing beside me, flashed a look up at me. There was real fear in her eyes, which I thought was understandable since if I'd been in her place, I'd have been thinking that the house had too many doors and windows for one police officer to watch.

"If you want," I said to her, "I'll stay here for the rest of the night. Then tomorrow morning I'll have a guy I know, Manny Fonseca, who's a good finish carpenter, come up and fix the front door so you won't know anything ever happened to it."

"Oh, we can't ask you to do that . . ." Julia's voice faded away.

"You didn't ask me, I volunteered. But it's up to you. I know you'd rather have somebody in the family do it, but your kinfolk are all gone away."

"Yes, stay," said Ivy. "I'd feel better. Then tomorrow we can decide what to do."

I looked at Lisa. "Is that okay, Chief?"

"No objections, but I'm still going to leave somebody outside. Ladies, we've been through this house from top to bottom, and whoever was here isn't here now, so you're in no danger any longer. You both did exactly the right thing and should be proud of yourselves. We're questioning the neighbors right now, and we'll have some people inside here dusting for prints. We may find a witness or lift a print, but even if we don't, we'll be making a thorough investigation, and we have a good chance of catching this guy."

And a good chance they wouldn't, but I'd have said the same thing she did if I'd been in her place.

"I'm certainly not going to be able to sleep," said Julia, "so I'm going to make myself some tea."

"I might have a shot of something in mine," said Ivy. "How about you, Mr. Jackson, and you, Chief Goldman? Tea?"

"Nothing for me, thanks," said Lisa.

"Call me J.W. I'll take the shot without the tea, if I have a choice."

"You have a choice," Ivy said with a small, crooked smile as she and Julia headed for the kitchen.

Some lab people came in and started to work, and Lisa stepped outside, glancing at the broken doorframe as she went. I followed her. It seemed as if every light in the neighborhood were on, and I could see a cop on the next-door porch talking with whoever lived there.

"Who are the Vegas brothers Mickey mentioned?" I asked.

Lisa gave me a sour look. "I'm surprised you never heard of them. The Vegas boys are two of the biggest, baddest scumbags on the island. Either one of them would make two of you. I thought we'd gotten rid of them years ago when they both went up to Cedar Junction for pretty good stretches. But thanks to the parole board, they're back home again and worse than ever. The main difference is that stir was grad school for them, and Alberto, at least, is smarter than he was before. And since he's the brains of the family and Alexandro mostly does what he's told, they're both harder to nail.

"They've got a protection racket going, but we can't catch them at it because people are too scared to talk. So are their women, in spite of what these guys do to them. And they're a pair of racists to boot. Hate everybody with a skin darker than theirs. Hate about everybody else, too, for that matter."

"Sound like a pair of real winners."

"They make their money by slashing tires and smashing windshields and storefront windows, starting fires, kicking in doors, clubbing people from behind in alleys, and doing the other strong-arm stuff you mostly see in cities. Then they go around and collect money so it won't happen to their customers again. You know the game.

"And just for fun, Alexandro's beaten the shit out of several people in barroom brawls, but we can't do much about it because the other guy always swings first. Alexandro Vegas has a mouth like a cesspool and the other guys are drunk or let the words get to them. Alexandro is a tough cookie and likes to hurt people. He was a big, mean kid before he went up to Cedar Junction, but he was only a big kid and the real baddies in there worked him over so hard that he came back the best part of a psychopath. You stay away from both of them, if you have a choice. And if you don't have a choice, don't rile them or let them rile you because they'd as soon kick out your kidneys as look at you."

"You say they have women?"

"Alberto is even married to one of his. She never divorced him, and when he came home from the slammer, he started beating her up just the way he did before they took him away. She won't get a restraining order against him. Says it would only make him worse. She could be right."

"And Mickey thinks one of them was here tonight."

"It's not a bad guess. Alexandro, probably. He's bound to have seen these girls around town. I mean, how could any man miss seeing them? And Alexandro was in the Fireside earlier shooting off his mouth about black women who think they're God's gifts to the world and how they should be fucked till their eyeballs pop and then kicked off the steamer dock with rocks tied to their necks."

"That seems like enough to haul him in for this bit of work here."

"Oh, we'll haul him in, but a fat lot of good it will do. His current woman will swear that he was home in bed all night, peaceful as an angel. No, we'll need more than suspicions to nail Alexandro. I'm glad you're staying here for the night."

"How about the other brother? Alberto. Could it have been him?"

Lisa shrugged. "Alberto cares nothing about anything, but, like I say, he's got most of the Vegas brains. He controls things, including little brother Alexandro. As much as Alexandro can be controlled, that is. Alberto doesn't kick down doors anymore. He lets somebody else do the rough stuff these days. No, this is more Alexandro's style of work."

"Are you saying Alberto might have sent him to do the job?"

"I'd be more inclined to think that Alexandro did it on his own. He's a real head case."

"How come I never heard about these guys?"

She gave a little snort. "They only got back to the island last year. You didn't hear about them because you're not a cop anymore. If you still carried a badge, you'd have heard of them."

That was probably true. Cops, social workers, medical people, and schoolteachers know about the Vegases of the world because they meet them or their victims, including their children and wives, every day. The rest of us never know such people. To us, they're almost unimaginable, although they're very real indeed.

And some of them live on Martha's Vineyard, that island paradise that draws one hundred thousand tourists to its golden shores every summer. They live under the rocks, like snakes in Eden, and every now and then one crawls out into the light, as the Vegas brothers had done. It's never a pretty sight.

6

By 2 A.M. the lab people had left, the Crandel house was quiet, and most of the neighbors had gone back to bed. I looked outside the front window at the cruiser parked by the curb. As I watched, the officer inside got out with his flashlight and started around the house. He'd circumnavigated the place about once every half hour since he'd gone on duty. I waited till he got back into his car before finishing the drink that Ivy had poured for me when she and Julia had served themselves tea. The women were still in the living room with me. They seemed wide-awake and yawning at the same time.

"Go to bed," I said to them. "Sleep in the same room if you want to, but go to bed. Things will look better in the morning."

"What about you?"

"I'll flop on the couch here."

Ivy's eyes flashed like dark fire. "I don't like having somebody doing this to me!"

"The cops are on the case," I said. "You can talk about it tomorrow and decide what you want to do."

"I spent a lot of summers here when I was little," said Julia. "This house is almost like home. I can't believe that stalker followed us all the way here. I hate him!"

She apparently hadn't heard about the Vegas boys being popular suspects with the local cops. "If he followed you all the way from California," I said, "he'll be a stranger in town, and the cops will have a good chance of spotting him since most of the summer people have cleared out by now."

"Do you really think so?"

"Sure. And I also think you two should get some sleep."

They went upstairs. I wondered if Ivy would sleep in the room with the words *nigger cunt* hacked and scratched on its door or would bunk in the next room with Julia for the night. Manny Fonseca could take care of that upstairs door, too, while he was here.

I turned off the lights and stood in the darkness looking out at the night, wondering why there were stalkers even while I knew there was no cosmic reason for their existence or for the existence of anything else. But even though there was no reason for anything, you didn't have to accept things. You could decide for yourself that some things were bad and others good, and you could work for the good as you saw it. Most people didn't have to go through that process, but I did, because I didn't believe in any of the gods or religions that gave other people solace and confidence in the significance of their lives and their values.

My world was just as beautiful and terrible as theirs, but it was also colder. It wasn't cruel, it just didn't care one way or the other, and I loved it beyond all things except Zee, Josh, and Diana.

Maudlin nighttime thoughts.

I walked around the house making sure all of the windows and doors on the ground floor were locked, then got a book about Oak Bluffs from a bookcase, lay down on the couch, and read.

Oak Bluffs, I was informed, had not become Oak Bluffs until the twentieth century; in 1907, to be precise. Before that it had been Cottage City, and before that it had been part of Edgartown until it successfully revolted and became its own town after the Civil War.

There hadn't been much of a population in the place before Methodism had become a popular religion in the early 1800s and had begun to enjoy several decades of evangelical success in the United States. All over the country, preachers speaking from pulpits set up in groves of trees attracted hundreds and then thousands of worshipers, who lived in tents and formed camp-meeting associations.

The Vineyard's camp meetings were some of the most popular of their time, since their participants could combine religious fervor with a vacation escape to a romantic island. By the mid-1800s, the Vineyard's camp-meeting tents were being replaced by prefabricated wooden houses adorned with gingerbread decorations, surrounding a central tabernacle. The tabernacle and houses still stand, perhaps the best-preserved examples of their architectural types in the country.

From the time of Stanley Crandel's supposed ancestor, preacher John Saunders, there had been a more or less integrated population in the area, including Azorians, Cape Verdeans, and others, and by the early twentieth century a number of black families and businesses had established themselves in the town. One of these families was, of course, the Crandel family, who had money even then and had built themselves the house that had later been expanded into the present rambling place.

As the new century progressed, the town had played host to an increasing number of upper- and middle-class black families, including some who, having money, bought places during the Great Depression and settled in. The end result was that Oak Bluffs became the premier black summer resort in the Northeast, complete with a beach called the Inkwell and an integrated population that contrasted sharply with that of most other island towns, which only much later began to include citizens other than Caucasians.

Just as in its early days, Oak Bluffs still lives off its tourists. It catered to them then and it caters to them now, bowing to day tourists coming off the passenger boats from Falmouth and Hyannis, offering them fast foods and Taiwanese-made Vineyard souvenirs that they can take back with them after their bus tours of the island. Circuit Avenue, the main drag, is a honky-tonk street full of noise and color. It sports several bars and restaurants including the Fireside, which is where a good portion of island fistfights still start.

The town is, in short, the opposite in looks, tradition, and temperament of Edgartown, which is sedate and, late in the twentieth century, still almost lily-white in both architecture and populace.

OB people like their place best.

I drifted off somewhere in the midst of a page and woke to find the book on the floor and morning light filling the room.

I looked at my watch. Six o'clock. I got up and worked the kinks out of my back. Down there where I carried a bullet against my spine, the last gift of a felon I had killed as I lay bleeding and frightened on the ground, I had a dull ache that made me worry in spite of my decision never to do that because it did no good. Doctors in Boston had left the slug there because they didn't want to risk crippling me. The operation, they said, would be more dangerous than the bullet, which would probably never move.

Probably. But every time I felt a pain in that area, I wondered.

It was early, but I thought Manny Fonseca would be up and around, so I called his house. He answered on the second ring, and I told him the situation and where to find the house. He said he'd be up right after breakfast and take care of things.

"Bring the strongest lock you have," I said.

"Sure," said Manny. "See you in an hour."

I went to the window and looked out. The cruiser was still at the curb, and the cop was sitting in the front seat. He was looking in his rearview mirror. I moved until I could see what he was looking at.

He was looking at a huge man who stood on the sidewalk at the edge of the lawn like something that time had forgotten, staring at the house. He wore a camouflage coat as big as a pup tent but none too big for him, and his face was the face of a creature that had not evolved from an age before humans could really be called that. His head seemed set in his wide, thick shoulders. He had no neck. His arms were huge and long, and hands the size of baseball gloves were knotted by his sides. His forehead was that of a giant Neanderthal, short and slanted over protruding, bony brows that shadowed eyes I could not see.

I felt the way I sometimes felt when I was a little boy, alone in our house with my sister when my father was out fighting a fire, and I heard the stairs creak at midnight. A monster was after me.

The cop spoke into his radio, then got out of the cruiser and faced the huge man, who, in turn, looked at him, then walked toward him. The cop, who was half his size, touched his holster, then took his hand away as the man seemed to laugh. I felt a chill of fear and pulled back from the window so as not to be seen or see what was going to happen.

Then contempt for that impulse stopped my retreat. I went to the front door and slid back the bolt and walked across the porch and down the walk to the street. The man turned his head and saw me and stopped and turned toward me.

I could see his eyes now. They were small and gray and merciless.

"You get some of that pussy in there?" asked the man. "How was it? You leave any for the rest of us?" His voice was something out of darkness. I thought of Grendel, the cannibal, who was descended from Cain and was doomed to hate and be miserable forever.

I looked at the cop. "You know this guy?" I asked him.

"Fucking piggy knows who I am all right," said the man. "Don't you, piggy? But who are you, little boy? Or maybe you're not a little boy at all; maybe you're a girly girl just like those two whores inside. You want a good fuck, girly girl? I bet you'd love it." He clutched his crotch with a huge hand. "Come to daddy." He rubbed himself and laughed.

"His name's Alexandro Vegas," said the cop, never taking his eyes off the man. "Don't worry about him. I've called backup."

"Backup." Vegas stared at me with his tiger's eyes. "Fucking backup won't do nobody no good here. We don't need no fucking backup here. Nigger bitches don't need no fucking backup. Not when I got a piece of ass like girly girl, here. She wants me to fuck her, don't you, girly girl? Come on, girly girl, we'll go someplace where we can have some, you know, privacy."

"You're not my type," I said.

"Oh, a dyke, eh? A tough dyke, are you? That's even better. I like to make a dyke beg for more cock. The tougher they are, the more I make them like it. Come on, dykie, we'll go home together."

"They took him and his brother into the station last night and questioned them," said the cop. "I don't know when he left there, but he just came here."

"What the hell do you know, piggy?" Vegas kept his eyes on me. "I could have been here all night and you wouldn't know. Fucking pigs don't see worth a fuck in the dark. What do you say, dykie? Let's go have a good time." He took a step forward.

The cop put a hand to his holster.

"You pull that piece, I'll shove it up your ass," said Vegas, not even looking at him as he took another step. "Come on, dykie. Let's go have some fun."

The sound of a siren came from the direction of the harbor. Vegas stopped.

"Looks like you get to go back to your cage alone, Alexandro," I said. "I guess you'll just have to screw yourself."

Hatred flared from him like a flame, but he didn't move. "You just made a mistake, asshole." He flicked his little eyes to my left hand. "You got a wifey, don't you, dykie? You got little kiddies, too, maybe? You got a house where you and wifey fuck all night and she stays with the brats all day while you go off to work? Save me some trouble and tell me who you are, so I can find them when I want to."

I was sick about the ring on my finger.

Two cruisers came up the street and pulled alongside.

"I'll find you," said Vegas. "I'll find out who you are." He turned away.

Lisa Goldman got out of the first cruiser. Three other police officers got out, too. "Hold it, Alexandro," said Lisa.

Vegas stopped.

Lisa looked at the young cop who'd been there all night. "What's going on, Larry? Trouble?"

"No trouble," said Vegas.

The young cop looked at me.

"Just talk," I said. "Alexandro likes to talk."

"He make any threats?" asked Lisa.

"He proposed marriage. I said I was already taken. He wanted to know who I was and where my family and I live. I didn't tell him."

"He didn't threaten you?"

I looked at Vegas. "He didn't say anything you can arrest him for, if that's what you mean."

Vegas grinned and spit on Lisa's shoe. "Oh, sorry, Chief. I didn't see your fucking foot there."

"Oh, that's all right, Alexandro," said Lisa. "Just hold it there for a minute." She wiped her shoe on Vegas's pant leg. "There. See? No problem." She looked at me. "You're sure he didn't say anything or do anything?"

"Well, he's smelling up the front yard, but I don't think you can arrest him for that."

Vegas stared at me with his animal eyes.

"Okay, Alexandro," said Lisa. "I guess you can go. And you and Alberto stay away from here."

Vegas looked at me a moment longer, and I felt poison enter my soul. "So long, dykie," he said, and walked away down the street.

Lisa looked at the young cop and said, "What happened, Larry?"

The cop told her, and when he was through, Lisa said, "You did right to call for backup."

"Yes, ma' am," said the cop.

Then Lisa looked at me. "And you did wrong. You just made yourself as bad an enemy as you can have. In fact, you made two enemies, because Alberto is worse than Alexandro. You should have stayed in the house."

My wedding ring caught the light of the early-morning sun and glowed against my skin. It was a bitter sight.

"Too late now," I said.

"Start being very careful," said Lisa. "And tell your wife to be careful, too."

I nodded. "Yes." My heart was pounding in my chest.

7

Manny Fonseca showed up a half hour later and looked at the front-door damage with interest. I told him what had happened.

"Guy who came through here must have been a real horse," he said. "That frame was solid oak."

"He's some kind of animal, all right." I took Manny upstairs to look at the bedroom door.

He read the words slashed in the wood and shook his head. "Jesus. You read about this stuff, but you never expect to see it."

"Can you fix these things up?"

"Oh, sure. I'll have to take this door back to the shop, but I'll have it back by tonight. I'll take care of the frame downstairs first. They know who did this?"

"They've got a suspect, but so far there's no proof."

Manny nodded, since he had friends who were cops and knew that lack of proof was a common problem for them. In most small towns and in some big ones, as soon as a crime is reported, the police have a pretty good idea who did it, since the same few people tend to be involved in most of the crimes; but proof is often lacking, so all the police can do is watch and wait and hope for a break. As the chief down in Edgartown had remarked on more than one occasion, if two or three families moved off Martha's Vineyard, his work would be cut in half.

Manny took the bedroom door off its hinges, and the two

of us carried it downstairs and out to his truck. Then he went to work on the front-door frame. It wasn't long before the noise roused Ivy and Julia.

They came downstairs looking swollen-eyed and tired; and who could blame them, considering the night they'd had? I introduced them to Manny, who, after the quick, hormonally induced stare that men can't seem to prevent when sighting beautiful women, even the swollen-eyed, tired kind, recovered himself and showed them what he was doing with the door.

"Have this thing fixed better than new in no time," he said. "You won't be able to tell that anything ever happened. Be stronger than before, too."

"Thank you," said Julia. "Can we get you something? Coffee?"

"Coffee black. I didn't get my usual gallon this morning, so I'm only at half speed."

I followed the women into the kitchen.

"Coffee?" asked Ivy.

"Black. While you've been wandering around town, did either of you happen to notice a guy, maybe two guys, built sort of like King Kong, eyeing you?"

They exchanged glances, and Ivy shrugged. "Guys look. That's the way they are. We don't pay much attention."

"You'd have noticed this guy, and if his brother was with him, you'd have noticed them for sure. Together they take up a whole sidewalk."

"I saw a great big guy like a gorilla," said Ivy. "Outside that bar. What do you call it . . . ?"

"The Fireside?"

"That's it. He came out and stood there, looking at us. He was wearing those camouflage clothes you see."

"He do anything or say anything?"

She gestured angrily. "We were across the street, but he put his hand on his crotch and rubbed himself. Then he gave me the finger. Another jerk!"

"You didn't tell me that," said Julia, glancing at Ivy while turning on the coffeemaker.

Ivy shrugged. "He was just another freak. There are a lot of them." Unlike Julia, I thought, Ivy's passions ran more to anger than to fear, and her performance at the Academy Awards ceremony became suddenly more understandable to me.

"I think you saw a guy named Alexandro Vegas," I said, "and he's not just another jerk. He may have been the guy who broke in here last night. He's a racist and a sexist and strong-arm man and maybe an extortionist. You stay clear of him. If he gives you any trouble, scream long and loud. The local cops would love to arrest him if they can find a reason."

"My God," said Julia. "What's with men like that?"

"His brother, Alberto, is supposed to be worse than Alexandro. They have a history of hurting people, including women, so don't try to be tough with them. Stay away from them, and yell for help if they even begin to give you trouble."

"That's the man who broke into the house last night?" asked Ivy.

"There's no proof, but he's at the top of the list of candidates."

"I hate this," said Julia, rubbing her hands together. "It's awful having to be afraid all of the time."

"Who's afraid?" snapped Ivy.

"You don't have to be afraid," I said to Julia. "You just have to be careful."

Her voice was angry. "You don't know what it's like. You're big and you're a man. Nobody is going to give you any trouble."

Zee had said the same thing, but I thought of Alexandro's size and comments earlier in the morning. He was willing and able to give me plenty of trouble. Anxious to do it, even. And I remembered the fear I'd felt.

"Maybe you're right. But be careful." I told them Manny's plan to take the bedroom door home with him. "He'll bring the door back this evening, so the house will be good as new by then."

"Maybe we should just leave," said Julia. "Go someplace else."

"No!" said Ivy. "Your family's been coming here for a hundred years. We're not going to let anybody run us off!"

"You can talk with Lisa Goldman," I said. "Maybe she can put somebody on the house at night. At least for a while."

"We will," Julia said. "But we can't expect her to delegate somebody to watch over us twenty-four hours a day."

True. "Maybe not, but she can have her people keep a special eye on you. She'd like nothing better than to catch the Vegas brothers breaking the law. It would give her a chance to put both of them away again."

Julia's eyes suddenly widened. "You don't suppose these Vegas brothers are working for Mackenzie Reed, do you?"

"Oh, no," said Ivy, pouring coffee. "That couldn't be. There's no way that could be."

"Maybe they met in jail or something."

"Mackenzie Reed is in jail in California," I said, "and the Vegas boys were up at Cedar Junction, here in Massachusetts. I can't see how there could be much of a link."

Julia was stubborn. "Maybe they're all on-line or something like that. Maybe prisoners have chats on the Internet, like other people do."

I had no idea what she was saying and told her so.

"Computers," she said, surprised. "You know, the Internet. The Web. All that stuff. They have ways to have chats when they're on-line. People all over the world can talk to each other. Didn't you ever do that?"

"I am the last person on earth without a computer. I just got a TV in the house a couple of years ago. You're talking to a Jurassic man."

"Oh. Well, people can do that. They can talk to each

other on the Internet, using computers. And I imagine that prisoners can talk to each other just like other people do. So maybe that's how Mackenzie Reed and these Vegas brothers got together. Maybe he hired them."

It sounded improbable but possible. What a world.

"I'll have a talk with Lisa Goldman," I said. "Maybe she can find out if something like that could have happened. But even if it didn't, and it probably didn't, you two keep away from Alexandro and his brother. They are all the bad news anybody needs, all by themselves. They don't need Mackenzie Reed or anybody else telling them to be mean."

I accepted my cup of coffee and we went out into the living room, where Julia gave Manny his cup. "How long are you going to be here?" I asked him.

"Should have this done in another hour or so."

"And you'll be back again this afternoon?"

"You got it."

"Good." I drank my coffee and turned to the two women. "You heard the man. He'll be here now and later, so you can relax. You look like you could use some more sleep, in fact, so you might try a nap. I'll stop by the station and have a chat with Lisa Goldman on my way home. Check out your on-line chat theory, among other things, and see if she's got enough people to put an officer up here nights."

"We can pay for a policeman, if that makes any difference," said Julia.

"I think that might make all the difference," I said. "In fact, the boys and girls may be standing in line for the job. It's the kind of work that's called a 'detail,' by the way. Like when you see a cop directing traffic in front of the Edgartown A & P. Cops love details because they make good money above and beyond their salaries. It'll cost you, though."

"We can afford it," said Julia.

And I bet myself that they could.

I got into the Land Cruiser and felt the Beretta against

my back, where I'd been carrying it in my belt under my T-shirt. I took it out and put it under the seat. Then I drove to the police station, which is right across the street from the ferry dock.

Unlike the almost brand-new Edgartown police station, which was big and roomy and modern and the envy of all the other town forces, the OB station was a pretty modest affair. I found Lisa Goldman, who looked a bit worn.

"I've been up all night," she said, "and I'm headed home to try to catch a glimpse of my husband and daughter before I go to bed. This business is playing hell with my family life."

"Cops don't have family lives," I said, "but Roger and Kayla will be glad to see you."

When his wife had gotten the OB job, Roger Goldman had happily abandoned his law practice and had become a charter boat captain. He worked out of Edgartown on the *Kayla,* a nice twenty-eight-footer named after their daughter, so he wouldn't present any possible conflict of interest for Lisa, who, as chief of police, might be obliged to take sides in some controversy regarding the use of the Oak Bluffs docks. In OB, controversy was the rule, so Roger kept his own business out of town.

Smart Roger.

"What can I do for you in the next five minutes?" asked Lisa, yawning.

I told her of the offer to pay an officer to keep watch over the house at night.

"No problem," said Lisa. "I'll take care of it."

Then I told her the on-line chat theory, and about the Mackenzie Reed situation, which she hadn't heard of before.

"I don't know enough about computers or about Cedar Junction to know if the guests up there in the gray-bar hotel can talk with their fellow felons in other parts of this great land of ours, but I'll check it out." She shook her head. "I'm way behind the times, I guess."

"Aren't we all. Another thing: some protection racketeers set up legit businesses and use legal contracts to collect money from their customers after they've scared them into paying up. Do the Vegas boys have an office?"

She leaned back in her chair and put her hands behind her neck. "But of course. They learned a lot up there in stir, especially Alberto. Their outfit is called Enterprise Management Corporation. They have an office about two doors up from the Fireside. Alberto's wife sits there all day, reading paperback romances. She opens up at nine and goes home at five so her husband can beat her up again if he feels like it. The kids run in the streets."

"They have a lawyer?"

"Of course they have a lawyer. Ben Krane."

Of course it would be Ben Krane. Ben Krane lived off the island's criminal minority, representing them in court and filing endless appeals, suits and countersuits, and whatever other paperwork lawyers use to clog up the local judicial system. In his spare time, he was a slumlord who owned several filthy and disintegrating houses that he rented to college students each summer for outrageous prices. He was thin and gray and totally immune to criticism. He was also very sharp.

I left the station and drove up Circuit Avenue. There, sure enough, was a door with the words Enterprise Management Corporation written on it in black letters edged with gold. It looked like the door led to stairs that went to an office above one of OB's cheapest gift shops. Ben Krane probably owned that, too.

I went on home. Oliver Underfoot and Velcro said they were glad to see me, but the house felt empty. I didn't mind, because I had a bad feeling about Alexandro Vegas and was glad that Zee and the kids were out of town.

The next morning, as I was eating breakfast, the phone rang. It was Manny Fonseca.

"You hear?" he asked.

"Hear what?"

"Somebody beat a cop nearly to death in Oak Bluffs last night. Kid named Larry something-or-other. You know him?"

8

"I know who he is," I said. "How'd it happen?"

"He was in his own garage, I guess. Still in uniform. Somebody broke him all up when he came home. Ribs, arms, legs, face. Stuck his pistol up into him when they were done. Jesus!"

"Where'd you get all this?"

"I saw Tony D'Agostine downtown."

Tony D'Agostine was a sergeant of police in Edgartown and not given to exaggeration.

"Thanks for telling me. Did you get both those doors fixed yesterday?"

Manny said he had. I rang off and called the Crandel house. Julia answered the phone in a cautious voice.

"J. W. Jackson," I said. "Just checking up on things. Any problems since last we met?"

"Oh, it's you. No, nothing's happened. We went to the beach in the afternoon. We saw that man Vegas when we came home, but he was a long way up the street, and all he did was look. And there was a policeman outside the house all night."

"Good. Just be careful, the same way you would if you were in the city, and you should be fine. If I can help you out in any way, let me know."

"Maybe you can." She hesitated. "Mr. Fonseca, the man who fixed our doors, said that you used to be a policeman and that sometimes you do things to help people. Is that right?"

"I haven't been a policeman for a long time."

"And he said you might be able to help us."

"If I can, I will."

But she surprised me. "I want you to investigate, to find out who's working for Mackenzie Reed. If this man Alexandro Vegas is working for him, I want to know it. And if he isn't, I need to know who is, because he isn't just hounding Ivy, he's scaring me, too. Ivy and I room together, and Jane Freed was my therapist before she was Ivy's."

I thought for about five seconds, then said, "I don't think I'm the person you want. I think you want a private detective agency. I can give you the name of a good one that's headquartered in Boston. Thornberry Security. They have a lot of people on the payroll, and they work on a national level. They'll give you your money's worth."

"I'll hire the Thornberry people if you think I should, but I already hired a private detective agency out in California, and they didn't find anything useful at all."

"Maybe there wasn't anything to find."

"Somebody is trying to hurt Ivy and me and our friends! I want to hire you to find out who it is. Mr. Fonseca says that you've done investigations for people, and that you're good at it."

"I'm not a private detective. I don't have a license to do this kind of work."

"I don't care if you have a license. I need somebody right now, right here! I talked with Mr. Fonseca, and I talked with Uncle Stanley and Aunt Betsy on the phone last night, and they say that I can trust you. I need somebody I can trust. I'll pay you whatever you want. Please."

I thought of the things Alexandro Vegas had said, and of what had happened to the young cop named Larry.

"I don't think I can help you," I said.

"Please.

"I don't think I—"

"Please! When we came home from the beach and saw that man way up the street, he wasn't just looking. I could feel his eyes inside my clothes!" Her voice had a shiver in it.

I hesitated some more, then said, "All right, I'll be up in an hour or so, and we can talk about it, at least. Have the coffee ready."

The world does not stop turning because people have problems, so before heading for OB, I finished eating, made sure the cats were fed, and mixed up a batch of bran muffin dough for future breakfasts. I have not yet met other muffins that can match mine, which are the kind made of dough you mix and then keep in the fridge until you need it. When you have a yen for muffins, you scoop out as much dough as you need and bake up a fresh batch. Delish! I put some of the dough into a plastic container for Julia and Ivy. They could use a little happiness in their lives. Then I drove to the Oak Bluffs police station.

As I went in, Roger Goldman was coming out, carrying Kayla. He and I had a common interest in having our kids around us as much as possible. He hadn't figured a way to take Kayla out when he had a fishing charter, but he was working on it.

"Hi, Kayla Frances Goldman," I said. "How are things?"

Kayla buried her face in her father's neck.

"Things could be better," said Roger. "Do you know anybody I can hire to shoot the Vegas brothers?"

"Just make sure you don't do it yourself. Lisa doesn't need a jailbird for a husband."

"I've got to go to work," he said angrily. He made a fist and shook it and walked on.

Lisa was in her office, looking older than before. I told her what Manny had told me, and about Alexandro's off-hand threat to shove Larry's gun up his ass.

"Sex seems to mean a lot to Alexandro," I said. "My impression is that he doesn't care if he does it with men, women, or goats."

Lisa nodded. "It's a weapon he likes. He used it against women before he went into prison, but now he'll fuck anything living or dead. It's all meanness for him. I think it's because he got screwed to a standstill up in Cedar Junction. The word is he got to be some people's girlfriend up there. He's a huge man, but he isn't as big as a dozen other guys who gang-banged him whenever they got horny. Since he got out, he's been getting even. Sex is a weapon he likes to use to humiliate people. We haven't been able to get anybody to testify against him, because the one time we had a woman who said she would, the woman's kid disappeared for two days and only came back when she changed her mind. The boy was raped before he was dropped off at her door, but couldn't say who did it because he'd been blindfolded all the time."

"I don't remember hearing about any kidnapping case."

"It never got into the papers. She never reported it officially, but she did talk to me after she got her boy back and told me she was dropping charges against Alexandro. Then she and the boy left the island. The story got circulated, and since then nobody's said a word against the Vegas boys. It's enough to make you either hang up your badge or become a vigilante."

I didn't think Lisa would do either, but her smooth, girlish face wore a bitter expression.

"Is that what happened to Larry?" I asked.

She shrugged. "It looks like he got home after the detail at the Crandel place last night. Tired, probably, and not paying attention. Somebody was waiting for him inside his own garage, probably hunkered down behind the pickup in the other stall. As near as we can figure it, whoever it was came up behind him with a sack and dropped it over his head, then beat the shit out of him with a crowbar and stuck his piece up his rear and left him there. We got a call saying something had happened. Muffled voice from a public phone in Vineyard Haven. We're trying to find out if anybody saw anyone at the phone, but so far no luck."

"Was he raped?"

Lisa looked at me. "Don't know yet. They've flown him up to Boston. He's in bad shape."

"Could he tell you anything?"

"He's in a coma. They say he may have permanent brain damage. It makes me sick. We'll pull Alexandro in again, but a fat lot of good it will do."

"If he raped Larry, maybe the semen will ID him."

"We'll see."

I left her there with her troubles, glad once again that I was no longer a policeman, and drove to the Crandel house.

There was now a peephole in the front door. More of Manny Fonseca's work, no doubt. Julia apparently looked through it before opening the door to my knock.

"Thanks for coming," she said. "Ivy's got your coffee waiting."

We went into the living room. Its large, comfortable chairs and couches, its Oriental rugs and filled bookshelves, its paintings and photographs of generations of Crandels, spoke of informal, genteel living, which was in sharp contrast to the tension in the air. Ivy Holiday was standing by the fireplace, her movie-star face bruised with a frown.

"You did come," she said. "I wasn't sure you would."

I pointed at a tray holding a coffeepot, cream and sugar, and cups. "I'll have one of those."

She poured and we all sipped.

"I may be able to help you while you're here on the island," I said, "but I don't think I can do much with regard to your admirer, Mackenzie Reed, because he's in a California hoosegow and I'm right here."

"You can find out if this Vegas man is working for him," said Julia.

"Maybe. The Vegas boys are bad news all by themselves. They don't need any help from Mackenzie Reed."

"Somebody is working for him," said Julia bitterly. "We can't go on not knowing who it might be. We need help. Somebody is out there."

I could imagine how she felt, and it may have been that imagination that moved my tongue. "All right," said my mouth, "I'll help you as best I can. There'll be some expenses."

"Don't worry about the expenses," said Julia. "Thank you." The women exchanged glances.

I was irked with myself. "Don't thank me yet." I took a slow sip of coffee. "I'll need names and telephone numbers of any lawyers the two of you have, and the PI outfit you hired out there, and I'll need to have both of you call them and tell them who I am so they'll talk to me."

"I'm not sure this is necessary," said Ivy. "It's probably just a waste of time and money. I'm not afraid of this Alexandro guy, and Mackenzie Reed's in prison, and maybe there's nobody else involved."

Julia had apparently heard that before, but she had the Crandel stubbornness. "You may not be worried, Ivy, but I think you should be. I'm going to do this!"

Ivy gave her a thoughtful look, then shrugged, shook her head, and smiled. "All right, if it's that important to you." Ivy glanced at her watch. "There's a three-hour time difference; we can make those calls as soon as people are up in L.A."

"And do the same with anybody else you think I might be able to get information from," I said.

"Maybe Buddy could help," said Julia.

"Who's Buddy?" I asked.

"My cousin," said Julia. "He's out there. He's working for an agency. He knows as much as we do about what's happened, and maybe he can help you find people who know more."

"He and I dated," said Ivy. "That's how I met Julia. Buddy and I broke up after a while, but we stayed friends. Okay, we'll phone Buddy, too. He knows lots of people out there."

Julia went to a wall and took down a photograph that was hanging there. She brought it to me and pointed at a face. "There. That's Buddy."

I looked at the face. It was a typical Crandel face, smooth and well boned. Smiling Buddy was standing beside smiling

Julia amid other smiling people who all looked Crandelish. I turned the photo over. It had been taken three years previously.

"That's my mom," said Julia, pointing to a woman who looked like a slightly younger version of Betsy Crandel. "And that's Aunt Anna, Buddy's mom. Buddy and I were going out to Hollywood, and Mom wanted a last picture of the family all together. Every time all of us kids are together, she wants one of these pictures, just in case we're never together again. She must have dozens of them stored away in boxes!"

"You leave your mom alone," said Ivy with a smile. "Besides, someday one of these pictures really will be the last one when you're all in the same place at the same time, and she'll have a picture of the historic event."

"Three years ago was the last time you were all together?" I asked.

Julia nodded. "The last time. We try to get together here every summer, but for the last couple of years somebody's always been missing." She pointed to young people in the photo. "My littlest brother is down in Washington sitting behind a desk in the Pentagon, and my sister, here, is in the Middle East now, working for the U.N. It's hard to coordinate all our vacations."

Julia put the photo back on its hook, and I finished my coffee and put my cup on the tray.

"Make your calls out to the Coast," I said. "I'll phone you about noon and get the names and addresses I need. And if I were you, I'd call Thornberry Security in Boston. Meanwhile, be careful."

I went out into the bright September day, wishing my thoughts were half so crisp and clear.

9

I drove up Circuit Avenue, so named, I've been told, because a century before, in camp-meeting days, it had been part of a circuit around the tabernacle, and, it being not only mid-morning but post–Labor Day, I found a parking spot without difficulty. It was right where I wanted it: a couple of slots down from the door to the office of Enterprise Manage-ment Corporation. I got out and tried the knob, but the door was still locked, so I walked up the street, got a *Globe,* and went back to the truck.

Circuit Avenue is a one-way street with diagonal parking, which causes a lot of traffic stops while people put on the brakes to wait for other people to back out of parking places. On the plus side for business owners, it allows for more cars to park near their establishments than would otherwise be the case; and for me it made for more comfortable spy-ing, since I didn't have to screw my head around so much in order to keep an eye on the Enterprise Management Cor-poration door while simultaneously reading my paper.

The news was about the same as usual. I wonder if it ever changes. In our house, Zee gets the sports page and the crossword and I get the rest, but when I'm alone, I read the whole thing, or at least I skim it, from end to end. I was in the business section, reading about the problems of some computer outfit, when a woman came down the street, unlocked the Enterprise Management door, and went in.

I read some more and watched to see if any barn-sized men were going to show up and do some morning office work. When none did, and I had finished the sports pages and noted that the Red Sox, out of the pennant race since June, were now on a winning streak linked, some writers were quick to suspect, to the players' upcoming winter contract negotiations, I got out and followed the woman through the door and upstairs.

On a closed door there the company name was written on opaque glass above the knob. There weren't any words asking me to Please Enter, but I did anyway.

Curtained windows looked out over Circuit Avenue. The windows were behind a none-too-young desk. Some file cabinets were against a wall beside a large, old-fashioned safe, and there was a table with some out-of-date magazines on it. Two chairs were in front of the desk and one behind it. In the one behind it was a woman reading a paperback romance novel.

On the cover of the novel was a picture of a woman with long blond hair and breasts about the size of her head that were bursting from a low-cut, white blouse. Her head was thrown back, her eyes were closed, and her mouth was open. She was being embraced by a muscular, bare-chested man with dark, curly locks and the face of a male model. Both of them looked a bit bored, I thought. The title of the book was *Love's Passionate* something-or-other. I couldn't make out the something-or-other because the woman's fingers covered part of the book cover.

The clothing and hair of the woman behind the desk were teetering on the brink of needing a washing, and her face was dull and sly. I thought it also carried a hint of a bruise on the left side. She turned down the corner of a page and closed the book, then looked at me without smiling.

"Hi," I said, sitting down.

"What can I do for you?" Her voice gave no indication of interest.

"My name is John Appleseed," I said tentatively. "I hope I've come to the right place."

She stared at me, then said, "What place is that?"

I put a fawning smile on my face. "I'm thinking of opening a business in town. Nothing big, you understand. A souvenir shop just up the street." I waved a vague hand in that direction. Another souvenir shop on Circuit Avenue was just what Oak Bluffs needed.

The woman waited and then said, "So?"

I turned my cap in my hands. "Well, I've been talking to some other merchants about doing business in town—you know, the sorts of problems that come up here, as they do in any town, of course, and I'm anxious to avoid them if I can, you understand. So before committing myself to this business opportunity I'm considering, I thought I'd do my best to take reasonable steps to minimize the possibility of having any unnecessary difficulties."

She said nothing.

I tugged on an ear. "So, as you might guess, I made inquiries to my fellow entrepreneurs as to how I might best accomplish that and have been told that your corporation has been most successful in assuring the smooth operation of local firms." I enlarged my smile and ran a hand across my brow. "So here I am, madam, to introduce myself and to discuss the possibility of doing business with your organization."

"I'm just the secretary. I don't write contracts. You need to see the boss for that. You got a card?"

I touched various pockets. "Heavens, I don't think I do. How silly!"

She sighed, opened a drawer, and got out a pen and a pad of paper. "What was your name, again?"

"Appleseed. John Appleseed."

"Address?"

I gave her the address of the house in Somerville where we'd lived long ago when I was young and my father was still alive and we'd vacation on the Vineyard when the bluefish were running.

"I have no address here on the island, you understand,

though of course I'll be living here if I decide to take that business opportunity, but for now . . . I came over on the early ferry this morning and will be going back this afternoon. Will it be possible, do you think, to meet . . . er . . . your boss before I leave? I've been told his name is . . ."

"Vegas. Alberto Vegas. You got a telephone number where he can reach you?"

I gave her our old Somerville number and said, "I won't be there until tonight, of course. Perhaps I can call you later today, before I have to leave? To possibly meet with Mr. Vegas?"

"He don't always come in."

I produced a worried little laugh. "Well, then, perhaps you can help me. I'm afraid I don't even know your name, ha, ha . . ."

"My name's Sylvia. But I don't do any of this business stuff. Like I say, I'm just the secretary. He'll call you."

"Dear me. I'm very anxious to meet him today, if possible."

"Why?" asked Sylvia, suddenly narrowing her eyes. "It's fall. The tourists won't be thick again till next summer. What's the rush?"

"Business, Sylvia, business. I have an opportunity to purchase a shop and that opportunity may pass me by if I don't act immediately. I'm sure you understand such things. May I have your card?"

She hesitated, then opened a drawer and rummaged around until she came up with a card. I took it. It looked like a normal business card, with the title of the company, an address and a phone number, and the name Alberto Vegas. At the bottom of the card, enclosed with quotation marks, was the phrase "Good Fortune Is Good Planning."

Cute.

I put the card in my pocket.

Just then there was a knock on the door and someone came into the room.

"Oh, it's you," said Sylvia, looking past me.

"Yes," said a voice I recognized. "I just came by to make my payment. I like to be on time."

The voice approached the desk on my left and I looked at the file cabinets on my right.

"I'll give you your receipt," said Sylvia, pulling one out of a desk drawer. A hand laid an envelope on the desk. It was a thick envelope.

"You'll want to count it, of course," said the hand's owner.

From the corner of my eye I saw Sylvia give me a sour glance. "That won't be necessary, Mr. Francis. If there are any problems, we can straighten them out later."

She scribbled out the receipt and gave it to Mr. Francis. As he bent to take it, he caught a glimpse of my face.

"Why, hello there, J.W. I didn't recognize you."

I turned toward him and gave him my best nervous but friendly look.

"Well, hello, Eddie. Imagine meeting you here." I put up a hand and shook his. We looked uneasily at each other.

"You know each other?" said Sylvia.

"Sure," I said. "Eddie's pizza is the best on the island. Right, Eddie?"

"Oh, yes, sir."

"You call him J.W., do you?" said Sylvia, speaking to him but looking at me.

"Initials stand for John Walker. But my friends all call me J.W."

"Is that a fact?" said Sylvia.

"So that's what they stand for," said Eddie. "I never knew." He put the receipt in his pocket and edged toward the door. "Well, Mrs. Vegas, I got to get back to the shop. See you around, J.W."

He went out.

I dangled my cap between my knees. "A nice fellow. I've known him for some time. Since before that kitchen fire that almost put him out of business last fall. He was lucky to be open again in time for the summer season. He called you Mrs. Vegas. Are you—"

"Started in a gas stove, as I recall. A valve or something."

"Yes. I read about it in the *Gazette*. I certainly couldn't afford any such interruption of my business. Did I tell you the name I have in mind? Appleseed's Arts and Souvenirs. What do you think of it? Has a nice ring, eh? It's a name people will remember and tell their friends about, don't you think?"

"Sure. You aren't a cop, are you?"

I pressed my knees together. "What? A policeman? Me? Of course not! Ha, ha. What an odd question. Good heavens. It's not that I don't like policemen, you understand, but . . . I mean, I'm a businessman . . ."

"Because if you're a cop, I want you to tell me right now." Her face was almost fierce. "If you lie about it, you're entrapping."

Ben Krane had been at work with his clients, apparently. The nervousness in my voice was not entirely feigned. "I assure you, Mrs. Vegas, that I am not!" I raised a trembling hand, as if under oath. "What a suggestion. I don't even like . . . that is . . ." I flicked an eye toward my wrist. "Oh, dear. How time flies. I have other errands to run, I'm afraid. Please tell Mr. Vegas of my visit, and that I will telephone you later today in hopes of seeing him before I have to go back to the mainland. Thank you for your time."

I went out of the office feeling her eyes in my back. Down on the street again, I walked up to Eddie's Pizza, where a sign claimed that the Vineyard's finest Italian food was served. I went through an empty dining room to the kitchen.

Eddie was there, talking to a man slicing vegetables. Eddie looked at me with surprised eyes. Then, as he saw something in my face, the surprise became wary worry.

I nodded toward the small office at the far end of the room. "I'd like to talk to you, Eddie."

He hesitated.

I smiled. "I won't take up much of your time."

Eddie rubbed his jaw, then said, "I think we're going to need more onions, Mark."

"Okay," said Mark.

I stood there.

"All right," said Eddie, and led the way to his office.

10

"What can I do for you?" asked Eddie, shutting the door behind us and putting a smile on his face.

I got right to it. "Can I see that receipt you got from Sylvia Vegas?"

Eddie's smile went away. "Hell no. That's my private business."

"You have a contract with Enterprise Management?"

"That's more of my business and none of yours! Jesus . . ."

"Eddie, I was there, remember? You came in and paid your bill and got a receipt and went out again. You weren't there to buy pizza dough."

Eddie pushed some papers around on his desk. "J.W., I got work to do. So I got a contract with Enterprise Management. So what? Half the businesses on this street got contracts with Enterprise, for God's sake."

"What do they do for you?"

"What do they do?"

"Yeah. What do they do for the money they get?"

He glanced at the door. "You know. It's a contract. They help people manage their businesses. Security, money management, making sure the health board is happy. That sort of thing. How to stay in business and make some money."

"How'd you make this month's payment? By check?"

"Of course by check. It's the only way to do business. Ask my accountant."

"Who's your accountant?"

He spread his hands. "Jesus, J.W., why are you asking me

all this stuff? You working for Lisa Goldman, or something?"

"Why do you think that, Eddie?"

Eddie ran a hand over his head. There wasn't much hair up there. "All these damn questions you're asking. Who you working for, J.W.?" He tried a laugh. "Maybe I ought to call my lawyer."

I narrowed my eyes. "I saw the envelope you gave to Sylvia Vegas. It was a pretty fat envelope. There was something in there besides a check."

He gave his head a small, violent shake. "No," he said in a rising voice, "it was just a check. I got to go back to work. Lunch people will be coming in. I don't have time to talk about this. Besides, none of it is anybody's business but mine! It sure as hell ain't any of yours, J.W."

He reached for the doorknob, then paused and took a lungful of air. "Look, J.W., I don't want any trouble with you or anybody else. I ain't no tough guy like Pete Warner. I want to be friends with everybody. But business is business and I don't want you putting your nose in mine. You understand?"

"Sure, I understand."

He nodded and put on a smile. "Good, good. No hard feelings, then. You come by one of these days with your wife and kids and have yourself a pizza on me. Okay?"

"Sure."

We went out through the kitchen, where Mark was slicing onions. At the door to the dining room we paused and I put my face close to Eddie's.

"You may be paying Enterprise Management by check so your official books will look okay, but you're also paying extra cash to Alberto Vegas. The payments will start getting bigger, and when you can't afford to make them, he'll give you credit. And when you can't pay that, he'll put a lien on the business. He'll own this place before he's through. Then what'll you do, Eddie?"

Eddie's face was thin and hot looking. "Get out. Get out of here."

I went out into the street, thinking about why Eddie had called Pete Warner tough. I thought I'd ask Pete.

Warner Electronics, out near the intersection of Circuit Avenue and Pennacook, was housed in an old wooden building. The main room was filled with electronic supplies and gear. There was an office to one side and a back room where Pete had a small repair shop. The repair shop was a sure sign that Pete was an old-timer. These days, most places that sold electric gadgets didn't fix broken items or, if they did, sent them away for repairs that took so long and cost so much that it was easier and cheaper to buy a new whatever-it-was than to have the old one fixed. Pete, on the other hand, would fix it if he could—and do it for a reasonable price.

I went in and found Pete. He was a leathery old guy who I'd first met at Wasque one day when we were the only ones there and there weren't any fish so we'd had time to drink coffee and gab. Later, when I needed what he had to sell, I'd done some business at his store.

"You need any help finding what you're looking for?" he now asked.

"I'm looking for you."

"Well, you've found me. What can I do for you?"

"I have a question I want to ask you. You don't want to answer it, don't. But I'd like to know."

"Now you got me curious. Shoot."

"How come Eddie Francis says you're tough?"

"Come again?"

"I was just talking to Eddie about his contract with Enterprise Management. He said he's not tough like you. Said he wants to be friends with everybody."

"Oh." A grim little smile lined Pete's face. "Well, I guess he says that because I've decided not to sign up with Enterprise. I guess that makes me tough. At least as far as Eddie is concerned, anyway." He looked at me over the glasses that had slipped down his nose. "Eddie is a nervous young feller, and there are a lot like him in town. Me, I'm not the nervous type. I never needed no help running this place so far, and I don't figure I will in the future." He paused. "Besides, I don't care for them Vegas boys. Didn't like their daddy, neither, for that matter."

A woman came up asking where he kept the extension cords, so he went off with her and I went home. I was glad we still had a few old guys like Pete around.

At home, silence rang through the empty rooms of our house. There had been a time when I hadn't minded such quiet at all, but that had been before I'd met Zee, and long before Joshua and Diana had arrived on the scene. Now, the quiet seemed cold and lifeless, as though I were living alone on the moon. Oliver Underfoot and Velcro rubbed against my legs, unaware that they were moon cats. Only a few more days and my family would be home again. Maybe I'd go over to the mainland and join them there. Maybe I'd go right now.

But instead I listened to the radio weather report and learned that Hurricane Elmer was still deciding which way to go, then opened the Yellow Pages and began to telephone accountants in alphabetical order. To each one of them I introduced myself as John Walker Appleseed and said that I was opening a business in Oak Bluffs. I said that Eddie Francis had mentioned this firm to me, that I was rushed at the moment, but that I'd like to call again tomorrow and make an appointment. They all said fine.

When I got to the *K*'s, I found Krane and Company and knew I should have gone there first. The woman who answered the phone said, "Oh, of course. Mr. Francis is one of our customers. We'll be glad to make an appointment with you, Mr. Appleseed."

I thanked her, then got a Sam Adams out of the fridge and took it up to the balcony. Out beyond the fall remains of the garden, across Sengekontacket Pond, and on the far side of the barrier beach, Nantucket Sound was dark blue against a pale blue sky. The water looked cold, although I knew it wasn't. Everything looked a little cold, in fact.

Fishermen were out there in boats, and surf casters were roaming the beaches, practicing for the Derby. None of them but Roger Goldman knew about what had happened and was still happening in Oak Bluffs. Their biggest worry, if they were worrying at all, was probably about Elmer. The fishermen didn't want a hurricane coming up this way because it would stir up the waters and mess up the Derby. The competition was tough enough without a storm making it worse.

There were, of course, contrary predictions about what Elmer was going to do. Since the Vineyard hadn't been hit by a really bad hurricane for quite a while, the glass-is-half-full people were pretty sure that Elmer wouldn't hit them this time either; the glass-is-half-empty people figured just the opposite, since in their view we were overdue to get smacked.

The *Shirley J.* was on her stake, and I was looking after John Skye's catboat, the *Mattie,* as well, so I didn't want any hurricanes visiting Edgartown. But not being into prophecy, I hadn't taken sides in any arguments about where Elmer might go. I was, however, keeping an eye on him, as were most other people who lived on the Atlantic Coast. When you live on the edge of the sea, you learn to keep a weather eye open.

But Elmer was far away, and Julia, Ivy, and the Vegas brothers were right here, so my priorities were pretty clear. I finished my beer, went downstairs, and got out my telephone book again. Sure enough, both Vegas brothers were listed there, just like normal people, complete with addresses. There was a third Vegas who also lived in Oak Bluffs: Cora. A relative? Mom, maybe?

I had about enough time to scout their places before getting in touch with Julie and Ivy, so I got into the Land Cruiser and went back to OB.

Big brother Alberto lived in a new house by the Lagoon, off Barnes Road. Pretty posh, I thought, and for sure not the house he'd grown up in. I drove past and took a good look. As I admired the manicured lawns and shrubbery, I realized that I was looking at the house on the bluff above the dock where I'd seen the *Invictus* tie up. Whatever Alberto did for a living, he got paid better than I did. Another American success story.

Alexandro's place, not too far away in a new development off County Road, was almost as big and just as new as Alberto's, but sported an unkempt lawn, a broken windowpane covered with cardboard, and an overflowing trash barrel out at the end of the driveway. Neatness was not Alexandro's specialty, apparently, nor was he concerned with maintaining neighborhood property values. As I eased by, a curtain moved in a window as someone eyed me from inside. Mrs. Vegas? Alexandro himself? The maid? I felt the eyes on my back as I drove away.

Cora Vegas lived in a hovel beside a dirt track that wound between other hovels that were surrounded by the unmistakable signs of poverty and despair: ruined mattresses, paper scraps, rusty pieces of machines, broken tools, worn-out tires, and soggy piles of unidentifiable stuff long since tossed out but never carried farther than the front yard. TV antennas were on top of most of the houses since cable had never made it this far, and there were cars and trucks as rusty as my own in driveways. It wasn't a scene found in the Chamber of Commerce's handouts or mentioned by the gossip columnists who recorded the comings and goings of the island's rich and famous.

I drove past Cora's house, found my way back to paved road, and went on to East Chop. There, after being eyed through the front-door peephole, I was let inside the Crandel house by Ivy, who looked quite smashing in shorts and a denim shirt.

"Oh, good," she said. "We were just going to call you.

We've talked to the detective agency and to my lawyer and they're expecting your calls. And here's Buddy's number, too. Maybe he can help you." She gave me a piece of paper with names and telephone numbers and looked up at me with those dark, evaluating eyes. "You know that I don't think much is going to come of this."

"You're probably right."

"We've decided to go up-island for the rest of the day. We're going to walk the Menemsha Hills trail, if we can find it. I know your wife's away. Would you like to come along?" A little smile played on her face, and I decided that Ivy liked men in her life.

"I'm afraid I can't make it. But I can tell you where to find the trail."

I told her that and wished them a fine day. I thought it was a good idea for the women to get out of town, where Alexandro wouldn't be likely to run into them, but I kept that thought to myself.

"Sorry you can't come along," said Ivy with perhaps a touch of annoyance in her voice.

I guessed that not many men said no to Ivy Holiday.

I drove to the police station.

"We're spending so much time together, people are beginning to talk," said Lisa Goldman when I poked my head into her office.

"If I divorce Zee and you divorce Roger, maybe we can get married and put a stop to all the gossip," I said. "Tell me: Is Cora Vegas any relation to Alexandro and Alberto?"

She cocked her head to one side. "The queen mother. Why do you ask?"

"I take it there's no king father?"

She shook her head. "Old Dino died some years back, and not a tear was shed by the law enforcement community. The boys inherited his genes, and just to make sure they grew up as rotten as he was, he beat them every day until they got big enough to beat him up instead. Nature and nurture working together to produce Alex and Albert. What a family."

"What kind of a person is Cora?"

"Cora is a sick old woman. Let it go at that. Why are you so interested in Cora?"

"I'm not interested in her. I just wanted to know how many Vegases I may have to put up with."

She leaned forward on her desk. "You stay away from all of them. They'll make mincemeat out of you."

"Maybe."

She pointed a trigger finger at me and shook it slowly back and forth. "Don't make any mistakes here, J.W. These guys do not care about anything. They will get you if you mess with them. If they can't get to you personally, they'll get to your house. They'll burn it down. They'll kill your dog, they'll torture your cat. They'll rape your wife and your children. These boys are very, very bad. Look what happened to Larry, for God's sake."

Her voice was as hard as her words, and although my hands were not trembling, I felt as if they were. I nodded. "Okay. I get the message."

"Make sure you do. I've been on these guys' case for a couple of years now, but I can't get to them. And now, my God, they've beaten one of my officers half to death and I can't even pin that on them. If they can beat a cop like that and get away with it, they won't think a thing about a civilian like you."

"You've made your point. I'll stay away from the Vegas boys. But in the meantime, the two girls up in the Crandel house are planning to go up-island for the day. Can you have somebody trail them out of town just to make sure that Alexandro doesn't follow them?"

Lisa sat back. "Sure. I'll have somebody escort them in an unmarked car. The girls won't even know they're being followed."

"Thanks."

"How long are they going to be on the island, do you know?"

I didn't. "A couple of weeks, maybe?"

"I'll be glad when they're gone."

I could agree with her about that.

I headed home to make calls to the West Coast, thinking about what Lisa had said and feeling more sympathy for Eddie than I had earlier in the day.

I thought of Zee and the children and was again glad they were away. Then I thought about how soon they'd be home and felt a knot forming behind my eyes. By the time I got home, my head was aching. I swallowed some aspirin, but they didn't help. I made my calls anyway, because such things must be done, headaches or not. Though Icarus fell, the farmer kept plowing and the ship sailed on.

11

Ivy's lawyer was named Herman Glick. Herman wasn't too happy to hear from me, but warmed up a bit as we went along. Lawyers are trained to be cagey, but can be almost human if you give them a chance. On Martha's Vineyard you can spot a lawyer at a hundred yards: they're the only people on the island wearing coats and ties. I don't know what they wear in California.

"Can you fax me copies of the letters from Mackenzie Reed?" I asked. "I don't have a fax, but there are some places on the island that do."

"I wouldn't want these to get into anybody else's hands," said Glick.

"I can understand that. But I'd like to see them." I told him where he could send them and asked him what he knew about them.

"Not much," he said. "Somehow he managed to get them out of prison and into the regular mail. They're all addressed to Ivy, and they read just like the ones he sent to her before he killed Dawn Dawson. The guy's a certifiable nut."

"What's he say in the letters?"

I could almost see his shrug. "That he loves her like no one has ever loved anybody before. That he knows she loves him, too. That no one can keep them apart. That her friends aren't really her friends, but her enemies. And he describes what they'll do together when she finally realizes that he and she are meant for each other. It gets pretty graphic. I'm not a shrink, but I'm told they're pretty classic letters. I guess Reed's a familiar type, as stalkers go."

I'd been in on the arrest of a stalker once when I was on the Boston PD and had later read about such people, trying to get a handle on them. Most of them didn't end up killing people, but it wasn't unusual, often taking the form of murder followed by suicide. Most of them seemed to believe that their victims either loved them or should. Shrinks had names and descriptions of different kinds of stalkers, but no useful explanations or cures.

So it goes. I didn't have any explanations or cures for anything humans did.

"Reed must have a colleague outside the walls," I said.

"For sure. The letters were mailed from L.A. I don't know how they got there."

"You've talked to the cops and the prison authorities?"

"Yes, of course. They don't know how he does it, either, or at least they haven't told me. And of course he says he isn't doing it. Lying bastard."

"If they knew, they'd probably tell you. Prisons can have pretty sophisticated communication systems. All it takes is a little friendliness or carelessness on the part of somebody working there."

"I know. I've read about drug lords still running their businesses from inside, and that sort of thing. Getting a letter out probably isn't too hard. Maybe his lawyer does it for him."

"He's got a lawyer?"

Glick laughed. "Everybody's got a lawyer, Mr. Jackson. Reed's is working his ass off, trying to get him a new trial. He's kept his face in the papers pretty well, doing it."

"You know the guy?"

"Name's Bill Calhoun. William Peterson Calhoun, also known as Wild Bill. Pretty well known out in these parts. Loves a lost cause, especially if the police work has been sloppy and there's some money to be made."

"Is there money to be made in this case?"

"Mackenzie Reed's old man owns a lot of timber and mills up north, and Mackenzie is his only child."

"What can you tell me about Calhoun?"

Glick's voice became cautious. "What do you mean?"

"I mean, is he honest? Can you trust him?"

There was a time of silence at the far end of the line. Then Glick said, "Yeah. I'd say you could trust him. That's not to say he wouldn't cut your throat in court, of course."

Of course not. "I'd like to talk to him. Do you think he'll talk with me?"

Glick was instantly cool. "Why do you want to talk with Calhoun? He's representing the man who tried to kill Ivy, remember?"

"He might tell me if he smuggled letters out of prison for Mackenzie Reed."

"Fat chance of that!"

"Well, you may be right. On the other hand, maybe he'll tell me something else that you and I don't know yet."

"It wouldn't surprise me that he knows a lot we don't know, but if it's something that might be detrimental to his client, he sure as hell won't tell you about it."

"Will you give me his telephone number?"

"I don't think it'll do any good. I don't think he'll tell you anything. Hell, he might not even take your call."

"I'll get the number from somebody else, if I have to. It'll save me some time if you give it to me. And could you fax those letters to me today? I'd like to look at them as soon as possible. And one other thing: if you have any of Reed's earlier letters, I'd like to see copies of them, too, so I can compare the early ones with these late ones. Can you do that?"

"I don't like it, but I can do it," said Glick sourly, and he gave me Calhoun's number.

"Thanks. We'll talk again later."

"Swell," said Glick, and the phone clicked and buzzed in my ear.

I dialed Western Security Services and asked for Peter Brown. Julia Crandel was going to have some pretty good sized phone and fax bills to pay, but maybe she could afford them.

Peter Brown's voice was muffled.

"It sounds like you're eating lunch," I said after giving him my name.

"Doughnut. It may be lunchtime where you are, but it's only nine-thirty A.M. here. Ivy Holiday called just as I got in. Says you're her man back East. What's your agency?"

"I don't have a license. I was a cop once, and Ivy's roommate, Julia Crandel, asked me to work for her. For both her and Ivy, I guess you could say. I think I've talked them into hiring Thornberry Security up in Boston, but she wants me, too, so here I am."

"Thornberry, eh? That's a pretty big outfit. Why do they need you and them when Ivy's already got me?"

"I think Julia thinks she does because I know the Vineyard, where she and Ivy are staying right now, and because I'm close and a known quantity. I suggested Thornberry because I know them and I don't know Western Security. Are you and I going to be able to do business?"

He sighed. "Ivy says we are, so I guess we are. What can I do for you?"

"First, let me tell you what's going on back here." I did that while he listened.

When I was through, he said, "Well, well. And they think Mackenzie Reed is still after them back there. It sounds more like your local racist hood, to me. Vegas, is it?"

"That's the name. The brothers from hell, from everything I hear. But they're the cops' problem; Mackenzie Reed is mine. I'd like to know what you know about the case, especially about what's happened since Reed got put away."

"The killing and the hit-and-run, you mean."

"And the letters that keep coming. I'd like a summary of

what you know right now, and then you can fax more stuff to me here, if you need to." I gave him the same fax address I'd given Glick.

"Remember when there weren't any fax machines?" said Brown. "No computers, no E-mail, none of that electronic stuff? Remember the good old days?"

"You can have the good old days. I prefer now."

"Me, too. Okay, let's start at the beginning. I wasn't involved then, but I've read the records and talked to people."

The beginning was about Mackenzie Reed. He was the only child of a moneyed lumbering family in northern California and had, by his own admission, fallen for Ivy Holiday after seeing her in one of her movies. Since he had money and didn't need to spend time working, he had devoted his life to winning the love he was sure she'd give him once she really knew him. She'd moved, but he'd always found her again; he wrote her letters every day; she'd changed her telephone number and kept it unlisted, but he'd found it again and had called her again and again. She'd gotten a restraining order against him, but he'd stayed after her, just outside the limits of the order.

Then he'd killed Dawn Dawson and been caught literally red-handed and had gone to jail in spite of William Peterson Calhoun and a couple more of the best high-powered attorneys his father's money could buy.

"And that seemed that," said Peter Brown. "But then the letters started coming again and Jane Freed got killed and I entered the picture."

"And?"

"And nothing. I went back over Reed's records. I talked to everyone I could think of to talk to."

"Jane Freed's friends and enemies?"

"Yeah. And her patients, too, those of them who would talk to me."

"How'd you get that list?"

He never missed a beat. "Hey, I'm a licensed private investigator. I get paid for being smart. Anyway, I talked to everybody it made sense to talk to and didn't come up with a thing to explain how the letters were getting out or who knocked off Jane Freed. The cops say it was probably a drug robbery gone wrong, and everything I've seen says that they're right. She caught some dope head in her office and he bashed her head in. Like the man says, the obvious is usually right. They may get him eventually, when he makes another mistake or one of his pals talks."

A lot of criminals are caught because they talk about their crimes and whomever they talk to talks to somebody else and finally it's a cop who's listening. If most perps were smart enough to keep their mouths shut, a lot fewer crimes would be solved. Fortunately for the police, most criminals are pretty stupid.

"How about Ivy's friends and enemies?" I asked.

"Yeah, I talked to them, too, just in case one of them was a mad killer or worked for Mackenzie Reed or knew somebody else who was or did. Nothing. Bunch of Hollywood yuppie types, mostly, or people on the fringes. A little nutty as a class, maybe—you'd have to be nutty to do that kind of work, you ask me—but nobody who caught my eye or smelled funny."

"You check out Julia Crandel and her cousin Buddy?"

He knew why I was asking such questions. Most killers are family or friends or at least acquaintances of the victims. We often get killed by people we know. Strangers may scare us, but it's the people we love who are dangerous.

"Buddy Crandel is a kid Ivy dated before all this happened," said Brown. "He works for a talent agency here in town. He was dating Dawn Dawson when Dawn got killed, so he would have been a logical suspect in her murder if we didn't have Mackenzie Reed caught in the act. I checked Crandel out pretty good anyway, but he came up clean. He was out of town when Reed killed the girl.

"And Julia Crandel is just as clean. Or if she isn't, she's the slickest little number I've ever come across. She and Ivy are very close, and I read Julia as being the genuine article. She's more scared for Ivy than Ivy is herself."

"Lot of dead ends."

"You got that right. If it was my money, I wouldn't be paying me to stay on this job, but it's Ivy's money so I'm still on the payroll."

I liked Brown's attitude. "What about Reed's family? Any of them likely to be in on all this with him? Smuggling out the letters, for instance?"

"There's only his parents. They say he's innocent, and they're still spending a lot of money to get him out of jail, but if they're killing people for him or helping him mail those letters, I haven't seen any sign of it. They're a couple of middle-aged rich people living up in Eureka. The old man's a bit stove up from some logging accident years ago, and the wife's right there with him night and day."

"Maybe they hired somebody. Sounds like they could afford it."

"They could afford it, all right, but there's no reason to think that they did. They seem to be pretty ordinary people."

"But you're checking it out, just the same."

"That and going back over everything I've already done."

"What about the landlord getting hit by that car?"

"What was it that Bond said? Once is chance, twice is coincidence, three times is enemy action? That sounds pretty good, but I don't see any tie-in between the hit-and-run and any of these other things. Some guy stole his car and Dick Hawkins tried to stop it and got himself run over and almost killed. The car was found a couple of miles away in the parking lot of a shopping mall. No prints except Hawkins's, and nobody saw who parked the car in the lot."

"So, it's a wash. The killing and the hit-and-run are just coincidental."

"Unless you're James Bond."

I wasn't James Bond, for sure.

"If you have any reports or files or summaries that you can share with me, I'd like to see them," I said. "Just in case I forgot to ask you something that's in there."

"Sure. Some stuff you won't get, of course."

"Of course. But I want whatever isn't confidential."

"You'll get that. You find anything useful at your end, let me know."

"I will. One thing more. Can you find out if Mackenzie Reed ever had any contact with Alberto or Alexandro Vegas? Maybe a mutual prison acquaintance, or someone like that?"

"Mackenzie may be a killer, but he's a yuppie. I don't think he hangs out with real hard cases like the Vegas boys."

"In the gray-bar hotel you don't always get to choose who you hang out with."

Brown grunted. "True enough. I'll check it out. At least it'll be something I haven't done once already. When I'm not doing that, I'll be going over everything else one more time, just in case I missed something. The exciting life of a PI. I don't think they're going to make a TV series based on my career."

"Another fortune slipped through your fingers." I hung up and found Buddy Crandel's number. As I reached for the phone again, it rang. I picked it up.

"Hello," I said, thinking it might be Zee.

But it wasn't Zee.

"I'm calling Johnny Appleseed," said a masculine voice. "Is that you, Johnny?"

I felt a chill run through me. "I'm afraid you have the wrong number."

"Oh, I don't think so, Johnny. Just wanted to make sure you were home. Be seeing you."

The phone clicked and buzzed in my ear.

12

They'd found me through Eddie, of course. Maybe on purpose, maybe by accident. It probably went something like, "Hey, Eddie, how long have you known this Appleseed guy?"

"Who?"

"Appleseed. The guy up in the office this morning."

"Appleseed? The only guy I saw up there was J. W. Jackson."

And the Vegas boys would have wondered why Jackson had lied to them, and what he was doing snooping in their office pretending to be somebody else. Especially when a little more digging could well have revealed that J. W. Jackson was also the guy who'd been out at the Crandel house when Alexandro had showed up there.

Like Mother Nature, the Vegas boys wouldn't like being fooled. They would have looked in the phone book, and they would have learned that I lived in Edgartown, off the Vineyard Haven road. And then one of them called, just so I'd know that they knew.

Be seeing you, the caller'd said.

I thought it was probably Alberto, because it hadn't sounded like Alexandro's voice.

My stomach felt a little wishy-washy as I thought about it. My address was no secret, but I was sorry that the Vegas boys had it. I thought of Larry, the cop, who'd come home from work, just as he'd come home a thousand times before, and had been beaten to a pulp in his own garage.

His home had ceased being his castle; it had offered no protection against his enemies.

A lot of violence happens inside homes. More probably than anywhere else, because that's where people live. Husbands beating wives; boyfriends raping girlfriends; children robbing their parents; parents beating or killing their children; friends killing each other over card games. The papers were full of such stories, and every cop knew that calls to break up domestic arguments were among the most dangerous calls the police could get. Better a bank robbery than a domestic, because you never knew what you'd find or who might take a knife to you. Often, it was the victim who turned on you. You never knew.

But I didn't want any violence at my house. Not ever. Especially not when Zee and the babies might get caught up in it.

I looked across the room at my gun cabinet, where my father's 30.06 and his shotguns were locked away, along with the old police .38 that I'd carried when I'd been on the Boston PD and the customized .45 semiauto that Zee shot in competition. A lot of firepower was there, and it could be used against us by anyone who broke into the house when we were gone and then waited for us to come home. For the first time in longer than I could remember, I was acutely conscious of the cabinet and its contents as a danger.

I thought of how Manny Fonseca always went heeled in spite of there being no reason to because, as he was fond of saying, it was better to have his pistol and not need it than to need it and not have it.

This old NRA phrase usually struck me as pretty nonsensical, but as I held the buzzing phone in my hand, it seemed to be a bit of wisdom.

The telephone in my hand seemed to be looking at me, as if to ask if I was through with it or not. I stared back at it, willing my unruly feelings away. Fear gives rise to hate, and

I was close to hating Alberto Vegas, a man I'd never even met, and I didn't like having that happen to me.

I told myself to deal with reality instead of imagined events and dialed the number I'd been given for Julia's cousin Buddy.

I listened to his phone ringing and then to the answering machine. A man's voice told me that I'd reached the number I'd been dialing and that if I left a message, he'd return my call as soon as possible.

I left my name and my phone number and asked him to get back to me.

I had no idea what Buddy Crandel might be able to tell me about Mackenzie Reed's fixation on Ivy or about the violence that had driven her and Julia from California to the Vineyard, but it was possible that he might know something that would give me a line on things.

I rang off and phoned William Peterson Calhoun, also known as Wild Bill.

A woman answered the phone: "Calhoun, Searle, Carlson, Patt, and Smith."

"This is J. W. Jackson. Is Bill Calhoun there?"

A good secretary is a buffer between the boss and the people who want a hunk of his time. This one said, "Are you one of Mr. Calhoun's client's, Mr. Jackson?"

"No. His name was given to me. I may have some information concerning the Mackenzie Reed case. I'm calling from the East Coast."

"One moment, please."

The moment passed, and then a man's voice spoke, "This is Bill Calhoun. What can I do for you, Mr. Jackson?"

"Ivy Holiday and Julia Crandel are vacationing here on Martha's Vineyard. A man has broken into their house and attempted to attack them. There's a chance that the man suspected of the attack is known to your client Mackenzie Reed. I'm calling in hopes that you can confirm or deny that. His name is Alexandro Vegas."

"You've misrepresented yourself, Mr. Jackson. That information has nothing to do with Mackenzie Reed. I'll give you thirty seconds to tell me something that interests me."

"Alexandro Vegas is a large, violent man who takes considerable pleasure in hurting people. Among other things, he's suspected of beating a local cop nearly to death. He's also a racist who seems fixated on sex and on insulting and harming women, especially attractive black women such as Ivy Holiday and Julia Crandel. If he was on the West Coast at the time when Dawn Dawson was killed, he'd be on my suspect list. Does that interest you, Mr. Calhoun?"

"Are you a police officer, Mr. Jackson? What's your interest in this matter?"

"I'm just a civilian like yourself, Mr. Calhoun. Do I have your ear?"

"For another thirty seconds, at least. You can begin by telling me if the Vegas person *was* on the West Coast at the time Dawn Dawson was murdered."

"Information flows both ways, Mr. Calhoun. I'll need some from you before we're through. As to whether Alexandro Vegas was out there or not, I don't know," I lied. "I thought maybe you or your client might know. If he was, it could be important to you. It could help get your client out of the slammer."

Wild Bill was silent for a moment, then said, "Why are you interested in my client?"

"I'm not. I'm interested in helping Julia Crandel and Ivy Holiday. They think your client tried to murder Ivy and is still trying, using some pal on the outside to do his work for him. I'm not so sure, but there's some reason to believe somebody is after Ivy and Julia and people around them, and if it's not your client, I'd like to know who it is."

"If anyone has tried to harm Miss Holiday, I assure you it is not and never has been my client. Mackenzie Reed is an innocent man."

"She still gets letters from him, even though he's in prison. Do you know how he manages to have them mailed?"

"My client does not write letters to Miss Holiday."

"He wrote a lot of them before the murder, and she's still getting them. All mailed from L.A."

"There's a copycat in Los Angeles, in that case, Mr. Jackson. Some of my client's letters were leaked to the local press and printed during the trial. Someone read them and is now sending his own to Miss Holiday. That someone is not my client. Are you a writer, Mr. Jackson? A journalist, perhaps?"

"No. And I don't have a tape recorder on this end, either. I've been told that you're an honest man, Mr. Calhoun. Are you telling me that Mackenzie Reed isn't writing letters to Ivy Holiday? And if you are, how do you know?"

"I am telling you that, Mr. Jackson. And I know because I know Mackenzie Reed. He is very confession prone, as you may know if you followed the trial. He admitted everything about his infatuation with Miss Holiday, and since then he's held nothing back from me. One of the hardest parts of my job, in fact, has been to keep him from telling everything to everyone. The most innocent of people can create a damaging image of himself if he says too much to the wrong listener."

True enough. The first advice any lawyer gives his client is to say nothing about the case to anyone.

On the other hand, Wild Bill Calhoun wouldn't be the first lawyer to have his client lie to him and get away with it. Lawyers, even sharp ones like Wild Bill, or maybe especially sharp ones like Wild Bill, full of their own vanity, can be conned like anyone else.

I thought I'd gotten about as much from Calhoun as I was going to get, so I said, "Well, thank you, Mr. Calhoun. One thing you might do is ask your client if he knows Alexandro Vegas or his brother, Alberto. If he does, it might give you a lead to follow. If it doesn't, it'll be one you don't have to follow."

I told him what I knew about the Vegas brothers, and what was suspected about them.

"Mackenzie Reed has never associated with such people," said Calhoun.

"He's probably associating with them now."

Calhoun was cool. "He's from a different social class. I'll look into the matter, of course, but I don't think anything will come of it."

"In that case, I'll have wasted your time, just as you thought I'd be doing. If you do find out something, though, will you let me know?"

"Perhaps."

"After you check me out?"

"Not before."

I gave him my address and telephone number, and we rang off. I didn't expect to hear from him again.

A copycat letter writer in L.A., eh? How many million people lived in L.A.? The town was big enough to house its share of crazies, no doubt, and it only took one.

Who? Why?

I phoned the Crandel house. Nobody home.

I phoned Thornberry Security in Boston and actually got through to Jason Thornberry, who'd left the Boston PD about the same time I had, but for different reasons. Thornberry had been a captain who had left to organize his own business, and I had been a foot soldier who left with a bullet against my spine, after a broken marriage.

"Mr. Jackson," said Thornberry. "Are you ready to go to work for me at last?"

It was a familiar query. "No, I still haven't caught all the fish and shellfish down here. When I do, I'll give you a ring."

"I notice that Elmer—what an odd name for a hurricane—seems to be bending up your way. You might want to keep an eye on him."

"I will. Have you been contacted by a woman named Julia Crandel? I suggested that she get in touch."

"Yes. She asked us to investigate the threats her friend Ivy Holiday's received, and we're providing bodyguards. There was a lot of competition for the last job, as you might imagine. A beautiful woman to be guarded on beautiful Martha's Vineyard sounds like prime duty to some of our people."

"Two beautiful women, as a matter of fact. Tell whoever you send that this isn't goof-off time. There are a couple of real badasses down here who don't care what they do or who they do it to."

"Thornberry Security people do not goof off on the job," said Thornberry coldly. "What's your interest in this matter?"

"I'm a temporary employee. Believe me, I'll be glad to step out of the situation as soon as your people step in."

"It's usually a wise decision to leave things to professionals," he replied in that slightly haughty voice I sometimes think he learned watching Basil Rathbone in old Errol Flynn movies. "I'll have my agent get in touch with you, to get your perspective on things."

"Fine."

I went outside and looked up at the September sky. It curved, pale blue, down to Nantucket Sound, where it met the dark fall waters. The sun was bright and the air was warm. There was no indication that Elmer, a couple of thousand miles south, might decide to head for New England, but . . .

I had a sudden sense that maybe I should haul the *Shirley J.* and John Skye's *Mattie* out of the water, just in case.

My prophetic intuitions are probably no better than those of most other people: I remember the times they were right but forget the many more times that they were wrong. Still, something directed me to pay attention to this one, so I backed the Land Cruiser to the boat trailer, hitched up, and drove down through beautiful Edgartown to Collins Beach. There, I unchained my dinghy from the bulwarks and rowed out to the *Shirley J.* I motored her in, dismasted her, and put her in my yard. Then I went back to the beach, got the *Mattie,* and put her in John Skye's barn. It took most of the afternoon, but when it was done, and I had latched the sliding barn doors, I felt better.

"Taking no chances, eh?" asked the chief of police, who happened along in a cruiser as I was lashing the *Mattie* to the trailer.

I shrugged.

"I think you're right," said the chief, stoking up his pipe and looking out at the harbor, where a lot of boats still hung on their moorings. "I pulled my own boat yesterday. The way I figure it, you can always put it back afterwards, if you want to." He gestured with his pipe to a trawler-hulled yacht moored out by the first green buoy. "You know that boat?"

I knew it instantly. Only one local boat was like the *Invictus.*

"Belongs to a guy you may have met up in Oak Bluffs," said the chief. "Name of Alberto Vegas."

I tied a last knot and looked out at the boat. "Never met him."

"You met his brother, though, or so Lisa Goldman tells me. You be careful, J.W. Those boys are mean."

"Meaner than me, for sure."

"For sure. Meaner than anybody on the island except, maybe, for Cousin Henry Bayles. Maybe even meaner than him."

"High praise, indeed."

"You watch yourself, J.W." The chief drove away. I looked after him. Meaner than Cousin Henry Bayles, the Crandel black sheep, was mean with a capital *M.*

13

I had seen Cousin Henry Bayles only once in my life, when my father and I were having ice cream on Circuit Avenue, and my father, who somehow knew who he was, had pointed him out. I looked and saw a scrawny little guy the color of coffee with cream. My father, who from time to time tried to teach me things he thought were important, had said, "Cousin Henry Bayles is a very dangerous guy, although he doesn't look like much. You should remember that many a big man has been laid in the dust by a guy half his size, and many an intellectual snob has been done in by somebody he took for a fool."

Years later, when I was with the Boston PD, I'd heard more about Cousin Henry from old-timers I worked with. The upshot was that if Stanley Crandel and most of his huge family represented the upper echelons of Oak Bluffs' African-American society, Cousin Henry Bayles represented the lower ones. The lowest, in fact. Cousin Henry had been a powerful force in the black Philadelphia mobs during the fifties, working first as an enforcer, then as a boss, before getting out of town just ahead of several volleys of machine gun bullets that left most of his gang dead in the streets and him on the run.

Or so I'd been told by the old guys on the force, although I don't think anyone in Boston knew what had really happened down in Philly. Cousin Henry had certainly never told anyone anything. Instead, he had come north, moved into a nondescript house in Oak Bluffs, and had more or less disappeared for a while.

Then, the story went, after a year or so, he was seen going off-island. A few days later, the new boss of the black rackets in Philly was blown to pieces when he started up the Lincoln parked in his garage, and after that, for several weeks, his gang members managed to get themselves killed in a variety of ways, including gunshots, fires, drownings, and knifings. Shortly after the last of these killings, Cousin Henry was seen returning to the Vineyard.

The old cops in Boston were surprised by only one thing: Henry's irritation with the black gang members. Normally, he only hated whites and other nonblacks.

In any case, Cousin Henry still lived in Oak Bluffs, but, if the chief was right, might no longer be the meanest man in town.

Or maybe he never really had been, for no one had ever actually proved that Henry had done a mean thing in his life. The only people who might have been able to give testimony were dead in Philadelphia, and since coming to Oak Bluffs, Cousin Henry had never broken a single law that anyone knew about.

Not that there wasn't speculation. On two occasions, particularly virulent white racists in town had hurriedly left the island never to return, and Cousin Henry had been suspected of being their propelling force. But no one knew for sure, because the racists had never told anyone why they'd left and Cousin Henry had spit in the eye of the only reporter (an Anglo-Saxon) who had dared ask him to give his side of the story.

Cousin Henry's exact words, according to the most popular version of the encounter, were "Fuck off, honky slime, 'fore I loose my dog on you! And don't come back, God damn your eyes!"

The reporter had beat a fast retreat and had not returned,

for one of the two known facts about Cousin Henry was that he owned a dog. The other was that he lived with a woman. It was not known if the dog was the kind you loosed on reporters, but no one wanted to find out. The woman, one of those people who might be thirty or seventy, was still seen around town, shopping or peering into store windows, usually alone but sometimes accompanied by Cousin Henry. Two smallish people, minding their own business and inviting no social contacts.

I had seen Cousin Henry in a Crandel photograph, but I hadn't seen him in person since I'd moved to the island and was now almost surprised to learn that he was even alive, since when I'd seen him that one time as a kid, he had seemed pretty old to me.

I wondered if the African-American community in Oak Bluffs was of such a nature that its members all knew one another. The wealthy and aristocratic Crandels knew about Cousin Henry, of course, because he was kin, but did other people? Aside from some degree of African ancestry (and Africa is a big continent, with native peoples quite different from one another), I couldn't imagine what they would have in common.

On the other hand, links between crime figures and the social elite were not unknown in Boston society, as I'd learned when a policeman in Bean Town, so maybe the same was true in Oak Bluffs.

Once again I realized that in spite of my years on the Vineyard, my ignorance of its people was nearly boundless. I could live here for a dozen lifetimes and still have more to learn about my neighbors. It was a kind of doom shared, I suspected, with most citizens of seemingly cozy communities. No wonder native Vineyarders, born and bred on the island, never saw any need to leave it and see the world. "Why should we go someplace else," they would ask, "when I won't live long enough to see everything that's right here?"

Why, indeed?

After getting the *Shirley J.* safely blocked up in our yard, I went back to Collins Beach and loaded my dinghy into the back of the Land Cruiser. Other people were also hauling their boats just in case Elmer made a run north. Hurricane tracks are notorious for being hard to predict, in spite of major advances in meteorology, and no one was sure where this latest storm would go. As is always the case when a hurricane is hanging out there beyond the darkening curve of the earth, there was a lot of camaraderie among the boat haulers. When confronted by such a common enemy, even men who might normally be unfriendly tend to set their enmity aside and work together.

I looked out at Alberto Vegas's trawler-hulled yacht. As yachts go, I liked the looks of this one. The stern of the boat swung toward me and I saw the name, *Invictus,* on the transom above the landing platform that crossed the stern just above the waterline. I was interested in the name because nothing I'd heard of Alberto Vegas had led me to think of him as being the type to thank the gods for his unconquerable soul or for anything else. More proof that my father had been right in advising me not to be misled by appearances or reputations.

Then I saw movement on the yacht. A man had come up from below and was climbing into a Boston Whaler that was tied alongside. He was young and bulky and looked enough like Alexandro so that I knew it was brother Alberto. I wondered if he'd phoned me from shore or from the boat. The brains of the Vegas family started the outboard and headed for the docks. If he sensed me watching him, he gave no sign of it.

Alberto handled his boat with ease and grace, and I wondered, not for the first time, why I sometimes presumed that graceful, capable people were somehow superior to most others in fundamental ways. I often had that feeling when I saw someone doing something well, even though I knew without doubt that such was not necessarily the case.

Of course the lovely ballerina might not be a beautiful person in any way other than as a dancer; of course the brilliant composer might well be an immoral lout; and of course, the ugly duckling was sometimes a swan.

I was not the first to flirt with the ancient notion that beauty is good and good is beautiful, nor would I be the last. Nor would I be the last to know it wasn't so.

Still, even after Alberto's Whaler disappeared on the far side of the yacht club, I was struck by the easy way he had handled himself swinging down from the deck of the *Invictus* and then bringing the boat into the docks, and I was aware of the ambiguity of my feelings: the meanest man in Oak Bluffs had looked quite handsome and attractive, and I suddenly thought that women might put up with a lot from him.

I got into the Land Cruiser and drove over to the parking lot at the foot of Main Street. There, I parked and walked to the dock, where Alberto was making the Whaler fast. He glanced up at me as I paused. His eyes were dark under dark brows, and they were without emotion. Dead eyes. The eyes of one who cared nothing for anything. His bones were just a shade finer than Alexandro's. His body was wide and his arms were thick and ropy. His hands moved swiftly and economically as he tied the last line.

"Nice boat," I said.

"Yeah." He picked up a plastic toolbox. "It gets me around."

"I mean the *Invictus*. I saw you come off of her."

He gave me a longer look with those dead man's eyes. "Thanks."

Up close I could see scars on his face and arms. Souvenirs of Cedar Junction?

"Looks new," I said. "Don't think I've seen her in Edgartown before."

"I keep her in Oak Bluffs."

"Strong-looking vessel."

"Trawler hull. She's strong, all right. Only kind of boat I'd own. I've got no use for a boat that won't take a beating and come back for more."

"I know what you mean."

"See ya." He walked past me and got into a brand-new Land Rover. Alberto bought only the best, apparently. I watched him drive away.

I took him to be in his late twenties. He was doing pretty well in business for a guy with his background. New house, new boat, new car. Maybe I should get into the extortion racket.

I followed him at a distance all the way to Oak Bluffs, where we went our separate ways. Mine went to the Crandel house.

Lights were on in the house and a car was parked in front of it. I parked behind the car and studied it for a moment. Two men were in it. I was pretty sure they were looking at me in rearview mirrors. As I got out, they got out. I didn't know either one of them. I started up the walk, and they joined me, one on either side.

"You have business here?" asked the one on my right.

He looked to be about thirty. An earth-colored man with curly hair, dressed in casual clothes. His partner looked much the same.

"I work for Julia Crandel. My name's Jackson. Who are you?"

"My name's Mills. This is Jack Harley." Mills took an ID card out of his shirt pocket. I looked at it. It said he was from Thornberry Security. "We're working for Miss Crandel, too. Do you have any identification, Mr. Jackson?"

I actually felt as if a weight had been removed from me. I dug out my driver's license. He looked at it and gave it back. He put out his hand. "The boss said you'd be around. Glad to meet you."

I shook hands with both of them.

"Tell us what's going on," said Harley.

We stood in front of the house and I told them what I knew. When I was through, Harley said, "The agency has some people working on the West Coast business, too, Mr. Jackson, so maybe you can just leave the whole thing to us and get back to your own life."

"Fine. I don't want any more to do with the Vegas boys. They're all yours now. The same goes for Mackenzie Reed." I looked at the house. "I'll just go in and say hi to Ivy and Julia and be on my way."

"They got home about an hour ago," said Mills. "We've all had a chat. One of us will be with them at all times. I think Jack's right. I think you can go home and leave this situation in our hands."

"Glad to." I had the little good feeling down inside me that you get when somebody tells you that you don't have to do a nasty job you never wanted to do in the first place, the feeling you get when you've unexpectedly been saved some grief.

I went up onto the porch and knocked on the door. Julia opened it and smiled. I went in.

"How was your day?" I asked.

"Beautiful," said Ivy. "We had the hills all to ourselves. It was like being a thousand miles from anybody else. Too bad you couldn't join us."

"Next time, maybe. I think Thornberry Security is pretty much on top of things here and in California, so I don't think you'll be needing me anymore. But if you do, you know where to find me."

"Thanks for everything," said Julia.

"You two relax and enjoy yourselves. Don't worry about the Vegas boys. I don't think they'll give you any more trouble."

"We'll have you over for supper before we go."

"I'll be here."

I went out and down the walk to where Mills and Harley were leaning against their car.

"The job's all yours," I said, meaning it. But then, as I started to go on to my car, my mouth, all by itself, surprised me by adding, "But I'd like to know how to get in touch with you if something comes up."

"You can beep us anytime, and we'll get back to you," said Mills. He gave me a card.

Beepers, yet. I was way behind in modern technology. Still, I was feeling pretty good and free, in spite of my meddlesome mouth.

"I may stop by sometime, just to see how things are going," I said.

"Fine," said Mills. We shook hands once again, and I climbed into the Land Cruiser, flicked on the headlights, and started for home through the darkening evening.

I stopped and picked up the mail at the box at the head of our driveway and glanced through the bills and junk mail to see if, by chance, Zee had sent me a letter, even though there was no reason to think she had, especially since she hadn't been away long enough for a letter to get to me if she had sent one. Besides, in a few more days she'd be home again.

I drove to the house between the darkening trees, my headlights reaching down the long, sandy driveway, illuminating it like moonlight.

As I parked in front of the house, I remembered Zee's pistol under the seat. Time to put it back in the gun case. I turned off the headlights and the engine, got out of the truck, leaned back in and got the pistol, and shut the door.

As I turned toward the house, I heard a soft sound and knew, too late, that I had been stupidly careless. A sack was jerked down over my head and cinched tight around my neck. I smelled the smell of canvas and knew that what had happened to Larry in Oak Bluffs was now going to happen to me and there was nothing I could do about it. I felt a terrible fear course through me.

— 14 —

But there *was* something I could do. I dropped to the ground and rolled under the Land Cruiser, taking a terrible but glancing blow from some weapon as I did. My left arm went dead, and I was blind and suffocating, but I rolled and scrambled to the far side of the truck.

Curses followed me. Another blow struck my right leg as my assailant knelt and swung his weapon at me. A baseball bat? A tire iron? A crowbar? Whatever it was, it sent a ball of pain up into my brain. My cry filled the smothering sack. I couldn't breath. I'm claustrophobic, and I was panicked. I had to get the canvas sack off my head. I heard the clang of metal on metal as my attacker swung his weapon at me again but this time hit the truck instead of me.

Then I remembered the pistol in my hand. I got my right arm free and fired the gun, not knowing where it was pointed, except that it wasn't pointed at me. The sound was huge and hurt my ears, but I switched aim a bit and fired again, trying to keep my shots more or less level with the ground. I fired again and heard the bullet bang into metal. Another hole in my already rusty truck. I fired yet again and heard a curse, then felt the earth tremble. Running feet? I shot toward the sound, then listened, with muffled, ringing ears. I was faint from panic and lack of air and forced myself to be quiet until the tremor in the earth ceased.

Had my attacker fled, or was he just waiting silently? I couldn't tell. But my claustrophobic panic couldn't be held in check much longer. I gathered my will and forced away my fear.

My left arm and right leg were afire with pain. I put the pistol on the ground and dug out my pocketknife with my right hand. I hooked the end of the handle under my belt and got a blade open with my good hand. The sack over my head was fastened around my neck with what seemed to be a strap of some kind. I got the blade of the knife under it and carefully cut it in two. Yet another argument for always keeping your knives sharp. I jerked the sack off my head and sucked in lungfuls of air. Life! I felt happier than I could ever remember feeling.

I lay there, breathing the sweet air until I had sated myself. Then I was quiet, listening and looking, hearing and seeing nothing as the night grew darker.

After a while, I closed the knife and slid it back in my pocket.

My arm and leg were hurting badly, but I ignored them and got the pistol back into my good hand. Then, moving slowly and listening hard, I slid out on the far side of the truck. I listened some more and tried to see through the darkness.

Nothing. No one. I got hold of the door handle and pulled myself to my feet. I looked and listened. Up by the highway I heard a car start and pull away. I put the pistol in my belt, opened the door of the truck, and got out the flashlight I kept there. I held it out at arm's length and turned it on. The beam showed nothing unusual in my yard.

I tried my hurt leg and found that it would support me. I edged carefully around the truck, sweeping the yard and house with the light. Nothing. I limped to the house and flicked on the switch for the outdoor lights. They flooded the yard. Nothing. I turned on the house lights, exchanged the flashlight for the pistol, and went from room to room. Nothing.

Whoever it had been was now gone.

When I was sure of that, I went out to the Land Cruiser,

where I discovered that by some miracle all four tires were still full of air in spite of my blind shooting, then drove one-handed to the emergency ward at the hospital.

An hour later I learned that I had a severely bruised leg and arm and a slightly cracked left humerus that wasn't serious enough for a cast, but was serious enough for a sling and some pain pills.

"I don't know about you, J.W.," said the young doctor, who had often worked with Zee in the ER. "Your wife goes off-island for a couple of days and you end up in the hospital right away. How did you survive before you met her?"

"I have always relied on the kindness of strangers."

"I don't think you should rely on the one who did this to you. You are going to report this to the police, aren't you?"

I had been thinking about that. "That would probably be the wise thing to do."

"Good." He shook his head. "I hope they get the guy. Do you have any idea who it was?"

"I never saw him."

"Maybe it was a her."

"I heard some cussing. It was a man's voice. If there was a woman there, she never said anything."

"Well, be careful. We have some violent people on this island. We see their work in here oftener than you might think."

That was no doubt true. The beaches, shops, hotels, sail-boats, sun, and summer sex that drew thousands of tourists to the Vineyard every year constituted only one of its Janus faces. The face not known to those tourists was that of many affluent resort communities: low pay and high prices for locals, few off-season jobs, and all of the problems associated with the resultant poverty.

"I'll be careful," I said.

"And don't use that arm any more than you have to."

"I won't."

He gave me some pills and a prescription, and I limped

out to the Land Cruiser and drove home. I hurt in several places and was filled with a deep anger I didn't make any effort to control. It was born from pain, fear, and frustration. Someone had tried to kill or at least maim me, and I thought I knew who it was. And the attack had happened in my own yard!

It was maddening and frightening and overwhelmingly personal. It hadn't been a public event, an attack on society, it had been completely private, an attack on *me*! And because it was so private, I wasn't at all sure I wanted to involve the police. Instead, the vision of personal vengeance gleamed bright and glorious.

My emotions boiled.

I drove down my long, dark driveway into the brightly lighted yard. I got Zee's pistol into my hand and went into and through the house, looking everywhere at once. Of course no one was there but Oliver Underfoot and Velcro, both wondering why they'd had to wait so long for their evening snacks. I snacked them, then realized I hadn't eaten anything myself for hours. I wasn't hungry, but forced myself to put together a sandwich. I had one beer as I ate, and then had another one.

I turned off the outside lights, then turned them on again. I turned off the inside lights. Now I could see out, but no one could see in.

I thought of how Jake Barnes had had trouble sleeping with the lights off and wondered—ye gods!—what I was becoming. I turned on the inside lights and turned off the outside ones. This was my house, and I wasn't going to let the Vegas brothers turn me into a prisoner in my own home.

Such vanity. Had she been there, Zee, I knew, would have asked how leaving the outside light on made me a prisoner. She would have pointed out that under the circumstances leaving the outside lights on was a sensible idea. Pragmatic Zee. Were women always more practical than men?

Then, as I thought of Zee and Joshua and Diana, I was

immediately awash in even greater anger and fear. The Vegas brothers could do terrible things to them.

But, no. I wouldn't let them get at my family. I'd kill them first!

I'd kill them first!

It wasn't a thought, but an emotion. It felt good. A world without Alberto and Alexandro would be better for everyone, not just my family, and I would be the instrument toward that end. There was even a moral charm to it. I would do unto them what they had done unto others and had tried to do unto me. The God of Paul might keep vengeance for Himself, but I didn't believe in God or Paul so I'd take care of the matter myself.

Oliver Underfoot wandered between my sandals and rubbed against an ankle, buzzing. He, too, was a killer, one who brought home his victims as presents for Zee and me. He brought mice, voles, birds, and chipmunks, had once brought a snake, and had once even brought us a tiny bat, although neither Zee nor I could figure out how he'd managed to catch a bat since we had never even seen one around the place.

He was simultaneously a natural born lover and buzzer and killer, a sweet, gentle cat who liked nothing better than a lap yet was a model for the cat song that Zee and I sang to the tune of "Folsom Prison Blues."

I picked him up and laid him over my shoulder. He purred. He was happy. Across the room, Velcro was cleaning her face after finishing her snack. Cleanliness was next to godliness in catland, too.

I held Oliver Underfoot. Maybe there was a God and It was a cat. If so, I imagined that the God found both killing and loving to be equally acceptable activities for Its creations. Certainly Oliver Underfoot and his kin were innocent hunter-killers. There was no moral component to their lives. They held no hatred for their victims, nor were hated by them. They were violent, but not vile.

But I wasn't a cat. I wasn't innocent.

I put Oliver down and went outside into the dark yard. Overhead, the Milky Way arched across the starry sky from northeast to southwest. A fingernail moon was off to the south. Four thousand years ago, people who had looked up at the night sky were building Stonehenge, and four thousand years in the future other people would be looking out there just as I was doing and would be building temples of their own. Throughout time, people have seen and will see manifestations of their gods in the sky, have sought and will seek the intent of those gods, the meaning of those stars.

But I saw no gods nor any import or significance in the stars. To me, the magnificent universe, for all its beauty and splendor and mystery, was meaningless and devoid of moral character. It was indifferent to the busy lives of such fleeting human forms of energy as the Vegas brothers and me. It took no heed of our hates and fears and cruelties, of our loves and kindnesses. It was, as old Bill observed, right as usual, "full of sound and fury, signifying nothing."

So killing the Vegas brothers was fine. The sun would still come up in the east, the tides would rise and fall, the stars would turn in the sky; nothing would change except that Alexandro and Alberto would no longer be around to terrorize other people.

I went up on the balcony and sat in the cool night air. On the far side of Nantucket Sound the lights of Cape Cod twinkled and gleamed. Human lights in cosmic darkness. Tiny dots that spoke of houses filled with people who had taken arms against that darkness and were living as well as they could inside the very cosmos that I found morally void.

The starry starry night filled my eyes and began to carry away my anger. I was alive and planned to stay that way as long as possible. I had Zee and Joshua and Diana to look after (although Zee would probably say that she needed no looking after and that she was quite capable of taking care of Josh and Diana, and me, too, if it came to that).

It seemed to me that my murderous impulses, however real, should be curbed if I could curb them. I wondered if I could. I willed them away. They didn't go. I willed harder. They looked at me with red eyes and sank down into my psyche. But they didn't leave. The red eyes still glittered down there and their forked tails lashed.

15

I woke in the morning tired and out of sorts after a night of tossing and turning. It was bad enough to be alone in our double bed, but my devils hadn't wandered off to someplace out of sight until almost daylight.

I made breakfast and listened to the radio. The news of the world sounded pretty much the same as it had yesterday. I suspect that we could stop listening or reading about the news for a year or so and not miss a lot. There would still be a crisis in the Middle East, famine in Africa, political unrest in Mexico and South America, and a plane crash. Republicans and Democrats would be blaming each other for economic and social problems, and unusual weather would prevail somewhere or other. Everything changes, nothing changes.

One change was that Hurricane Elmer was definitely heading northwest at the moment, although the weather people weren't making any real predictions about its eventual path. Bermuda was keeping an eye on the storm, as was North Carolina, because one never knows, do one?

No, one doesn't.

I did know one thing: my hope of being no longer involved with the problems in Oak Bluffs had been naive. The Vegas brothers and I still had business together, and through Alexandro I was also still tied to Ivy Holiday and Julia Crandel.

Because I didn't want Zee involved in all this, I cleaned her .380, reloaded its clip, and locked both in the gun cabinet.

Then, because I *was* involved, I loaded my old police .38 and took it out to the Land Cruiser and put it under the seat.

The canvas bag was lying on the ground where I'd thrown it last night. The crude but utilitarian homemade sack had the remains of a nylon strap around its neck. When the strap had been intact, you could yank it tight with one hand, and it stayed tight until you loosened it by manipulating the buckle.

Cute.

Something up the driveway caught my eye, and I walked up there and found my own two-foot crowbar. I guessed that my assailant had tossed it there as he retreated. He (she? they?) had gotten it out of the back shed and had used it to break my arm. My own crowbar.

Cute, again. The red-eyed demon showed his face. I ordered him back into his lair.

I gathered up the shell casings from the ground and tossed them into a rubbish barrel.

Oliver Underfoot and Velcro were hanging around, supervising. They liked watching their people do the strange things they did. They were very social cats.

"You're in charge," I said to them. "Keep an eye on things. Catch some mousies."

Then I drove to the Oak Bluffs police station.

A lot of police cars were parked there, and I knew why. A local cop had been beaten half to death, and cops look after their own. Even some off-island state police had come down and joined the investigation, and cops were there from other island towns.

It's one example of Vineyard nonsense (born of town rivalries) that ten separate police forces are on an island that has a winter population of only twelve thousand, but this time I didn't mind the absurdity. The more cops, the better, as long as they didn't get under one another's feet. Maybe the Vegas boys had finally gone a step too far and had gotten too many people mad at them.

I went in, carrying the sack and the crowbar, gave my name to the kid at the desk, and asked to see Lisa Goldman.

"She's busy." The kid was just a tad too conscious of being in a position to influence my life.

"She may not be too busy to see these." I held up my wares.

"Wait here, please." He went away and came back. "You can go on in."

I went into Lisa's office. A half dozen people were there, including Corporal Dominic Agganis and Officer Olive Otero, the island's state-police representatives, and Tony D'Agostine, of the Edgartown PD.

I put the crowbar and the canvas sack on Lisa's desk. She looked at them and at my sling.

"What happened to you?"

I told her, then said, "My prints will be on the crowbar, I don't know about his. I don't know if you can get prints off of the bag, but mine will be on there, too, if you can."

"You should have called 911," said Tony D'Agostine.

"You're right. But I didn't."

"We'd better get a detective to the crime scene," said Tony. "Maybe we can learn something. I'll use the phone at the desk." He went out.

"We'll send these to the lab," said Lisa. "Maybe we'll get lucky. Probably not. We didn't get any prints at Larry's place. Guy probably wore gloves."

Agganis said, "How do you fit into all this, J.W.? Why would somebody be this mad at you and Larry both?"

"If the somebody is one or both of the Vegas brothers, it might be because Larry and I both pissed off Alexandro Vegas up there at the Crandel place, and because Alexandro doesn't like being pissed off."

"How did he know who you were? Where you live?"

It was confession time. I told them about my visits to Alberto's office and to Eddie Francis's pizza place, about the phone call I'd gotten for John Appleseed, and about my theory that Eddie had given Alberto my name.

"Jesus," said Olive Otero, with whom I'd never gotten along too well, "you should probably be in jail. Interfering with a police investigation is a crime, as you damned well know."

She irked me, as usual. "What police investigation? I didn't interfere with any police investigation!"

"Well, if there was a law against stupidity, you'd be in the hoosegow for sure," said Agganis, shaking his head. "Johnny Appleseed, for God's sake. Couldn't you come up with a better moniker than that? Even Alberto Vegas and his wife must have smelled something funny when you gave them that name."

"It was the first name that came to mind. It just popped out."

"And just what were you doing in Alberto's office?" asked Olive, speaking with a curled lip. "What were you planning to do? Make your own investigation? Get the goods on the Vegas boys all by yourself since the cops are too dumb to do it, like in the movies? Is that it?"

I sneered back at her. "I was afraid they'd put you in charge of the investigation, Olive. I knew I had to do something before you screwed things up so badly they'd stay screwed forever."

"Oh, you did, eh?" Olive stepped toward me.

"Now, hold on," said Agganis, putting a thick arm out between us. "Don't let him get to you, Olive."

"Yeah," said Lisa, raising a hand in a gesture of peace. "Let's all hold on. We don't need any fighting among ourselves."

"He's not one of ourselves," said mad Olive. "I know he was a cop once, but now he's just a civilian. Get him out of here!"

Lisa looked at her. "Now, Olive," she said in her gentle voice. "Somebody attacked J.W. last night just like somebody attacked Larry. And J.W. is working for the women living in the Crandel house. And there may be a tie-in between what happened at the house and the assaults on Larry and J.W. So J.W. is involved even if he's not a policeman. Now, the more we all cooperate, the better off we'll be."

The sweet voice of reason didn't seem to have much effect on Olive. "I don't like his being involved," she said.

"But he is involved," said Agganis, "and that's that, Officer Otero." He had a small smile on his face as he spoke, but Olive got the message and shut her mouth.

I looked back at Lisa. "You know about the two bodyguards over at the Crandel place?"

She nodded. "Harley and Mills. They came by and introduced themselves so there wouldn't be any misunderstandings. All they're doing here is guarding the two women. They're not involved in any investigations."

"These guys may not be, but Thornberry Security is digging into the stalker case out on the Coast: the killings and the letters that are still coming even though Mackenzie Reed is in jail. Did you ever find out if there might be a tie-in between Reed and the Vegas boys?"

Lisa shook her head. "There's no indication that they had any contact or even knew about one another. Do you have reason to think there might be a tie-in? Anything we didn't talk about before?"

"No, but I talked to some people out there." I summarized my conversations with Glick, Brown, and Calhoun.

"I think the California stuff and our problems here are separate things," said Lisa. "But if they're not, I guess we shouldn't be surprised."

Very little in the way of crime surprises police officers.

Tony D'Agostine came back into the office. "J.W., you want to go back to your place and show us what happened where? We'll meet the detectives there."

"Sure."

Tony looked at Lisa. "Anything we can do to help, Chief,

you let us know. You need some extra hands, anything like that. You tell Larry that there's people praying for him."

"Thanks," said Lisa. "We'll stay in touch."

Tony and I went out, and I followed his cruiser back to my place. Another cruiser was already there, and Tom Flynn and Joy Look were standing beside it. There had been Flynns and Looks on the island for centuries, and these two current models were Edgartown's detectives.

Tony put his cruiser beside theirs, and I parked the Land Cruiser where I'd parked it the night before.

I told my tale once again and showed what had happened.

"Maybe you hit him when you shot," said Joy. "How many rounds did you use."

"I found five shell casings this morning."

"Where are they?"

"In the rubbish."

"Jesus, J.W., you know better than that."

I decided not to tell them that I'd given thought to not involving the police, but taking care of the Vegas boys on my own.

"I wasn't thinking very straight," I said.

"Ah, no matter," said Joy. "But dig them up for us, will you, and we'll put them into one of our little evidence bags. You think you may have hit the guy?"

"I couldn't see anything, so I don't know if I ever even got one near him."

"Well, we'll check things out as best we can. Maybe he dropped a matchbook with his name and address on it. Ha, ha!"

"Maybe he's in the hospital right now with a bullet in him," said Tom. "Maybe this will be an easy one."

Joy allowed herself another laugh.

I went to dig the shell casings out of the rubbish.

16

By noon, after the cops were gone, I was out of zip, in pain, and feeling sorry for myself. I wished Zee were there, but immediately was glad she wasn't. The rest of that day I lay naked out in the yard in the fall sunlight and gave nature a chance to burn away some of the hurt and self-pity that I was paying too much attention to. Between dozes I thought about the Vegas boys and their violent ways.

That night, I heard a fire horn blowing, calling the volunteers to their dangerous work. The sound lifted me out of my dreams and I stared at the dark ceiling of the bedroom and listened. Sure enough, the horn blew again, and I found myself thinking of the fire in Eddie Francis's kitchen. I had an impulse to get dressed and go find what was burning, but I knew the firemen didn't need any civilians hanging around getting in their way, so I stayed where I was.

In the morning, though, I phoned the emergency center. I recognized the voice at the other end as that of Sophie Fox, who was cheerful as usual.

"Oh, hi, J.W. What can I do for you?"

"I'm just calling to find out where the fire was last night."

"Up in OB. Private home. Warner place, off Newton Avenue. Nobody hurt, but I guess the house is a total loss."

The Warner place. "Pete Warner's place?"

"Yeah. You know him?"

I felt sick. "Yeah, I know him. Thanks, Sophie."

"Say hi to Zee."

"I will."

I climbed into the Land Cruiser and drove to the blinker, then followed Barnes Road to Linden Avenue. A sharp left and then a right took me to Newton Avenue, and not much later I came to a mailbox that said Warner. A driveway led toward Lagoon Pond and I could see the blackened remains of a house down near the water. A fire truck was there, and a police car, and people were standing and talking. One of them, shoulders slumped, looked like Pete. A woman about his age had her arm around his waist. I drove by and went on to the police station.

"If you're going to live here," said Lisa Goldman, "I'm going to have to start charging you rent." She was red eyed and looked tired.

"I just came by Pete Warner's place."

She leaned back in her chair. "Somebody torched his house last night."

"Torched?"

"Yeah. Arson. Pretty obvious. Whoever did it didn't make any attempt to hide it. Left the gas cans right there, like he wanted people to know it was no accident. You don't look surprised. You know something I don't know?"

"Probably not. I do know that the last time I talked with Pete, Warner Electronics didn't have a contract with Enterprise Management."

She put her fingertips together. "Are you telling me that the Vegas boys burned down Pete's house because he wouldn't do business with them? You'd better not say that in front of Ben Krane. He'll have your ass in court for slander."

"Ben Krane's outfit does Eddie Francis's accounting. I wonder if they do the accounting for everybody who's contracted to Enterprise Management. And how about insurance? Does Krane handle all their insurance, too? What do you think? You're a cop so you might ask around. If you want to make a friendly wager on what you'll find out, I'll bet you a six of Sam Adams that Krane does a lot of business with the people who've signed on with Enterprise."

"I won't take the bet, but I will ask around." She sat forward and rubbed her neck. "You know anybody wants a job?"

I was struck by the uncharacteristic mixture of fatigue and bitterness in her voice. "What do you mean?"

"Couple of my people are talking about quitting the force. They don't want what happened to Larry happening to them. Can't really blame them, but I can't afford to lose them either. Especially not right now when I need everybody I've got." She looked up at me. "I'll tell you something. If the Vegas boys don't get stopped pretty soon, this town is in trouble. Hell, we're already in trouble, and it's spreading to other towns."

"All these extra cops down here, maybe they'll find something. Maybe things will change."

"Yeah. Maybe." She drew a deep breath and seemed to will her despair away. "You seen the new visitor over at the Crandel place? Got in last night from the West Coast. Fella named Buddy Crandel. Cousin of Julia Crandel. He had a hard time getting past those two Thornberry men, I hear. The Crandel girl had to ID him before they'd let him in."

No wonder I hadn't gotten Crandel when I'd telephoned. He'd been on his way east. I looked at my watch.

"I'd like to talk with him," I said. "I think I'll go over there."

"Pretty early in the morning. Beauty sleep, and all that."

"If nobody's up, I'll wait till they are."

They weren't up, but I changed my mind about waiting. Instead, I drove down to the Edgartown police station. The chief was in his office, shuffling papers. He looked up at me.

"What do you want?"

I told him what Lisa Goldman had said about Oak Bluffs' troubles spreading to other towns. "I just wanted to know if any of that trouble had gotten this far."

"It's a small island. Infections spread fast."

"You mean the Vegas boys are selling protection in Edgartown, too?"

"'Selling protection' isn't the phrase Alberto and Alexandro would use. I think they'd call it contracting with Enterprise Management."

"What do you call it?"

"If I could prove anything, I'd call it extortion. But so far, I can't."

"Last year Eddie Francis wasn't signed up and had a kitchen fire. Now he's signed up. Pete Warner didn't sign up, and last night his house burned down. Larry Curtis stood up to Alexandro and got himself beaten to a pulp. The same thing almost happened to me. How much proof do you need?"

He raised a brow. "You willing to testify under oath that Alexandro Vegas attacked you? If you are, I'll get a warrant right now and arrest him."

"No. I didn't see who it was. But I know it was him."

"You don't know anything. And neither do I. Yet."

"Yet?"

"We're talking to all of the merchants and businessmen in town. Maybe some of them will work with us. But Alberto is slick. He never does anything illegal."

"Extortion is sure as hell illegal."

"Yeah, but he never threatens anybody. He goes into a store or office and tries to get the people who run the business to buy policies with his company. If they don't buy, he wishes them good luck, says he hopes they'll change their minds and that they won't mind if he drops by again sometime, and he leaves. Sometimes Alexandro goes with him, but he never says anything. He just stands there while Alberto talks and then leaves with him."

"Couldn't you argue that having Alexandro there is an implied threat?"

The chief smiled a chilly smile. "Try that in court and see how far you get."

I thought he was right, but I pushed the idea anyway. "What if some customer would testify that the sight of

Alexandro and the street gossip about what happens to people who don't do business with Alberto frightened him into signing up with Enterprise Management?"

The chief shrugged. "I'm no lawyer, but I don't think just having somebody say he was scared would be enough. I think there has to be an overt threat. And so far, there hasn't been."

"At least none that anybody'll talk about. And the next step in the master plan, if you're right about Alberto and Alexandro, is that somebody's store catches on fire, or somebody gets sugar dumped in the gas tanks of his equipment, or the place is vandalized."

The chief nodded. "Yeah. And a couple of days later Alberto shows up again and says how sorry he is about the accident and gives them another chance to buy a policy from him. If they do, fine; if they don't, well, sometimes later on there's another accident." Then, before I could say what came to my mind, the chief waved a forefinger at me and went on, "But there isn't always an accident. Sometimes after somebody says no, nothing happens to them at all."

Sly Alberto. If there was always an accident after a failed attempt to sell a policy, the obvious pattern might persuade a judge or jury that there was, indeed, an extortion racket going on. But if accidents only happened sometimes, it would be a hard case to make.

"Who does the dirty work after somebody says no?" I asked.

"Who knows? Alexandro, I'd guess. But so far nobody's ever caught him at it."

"Last night whoever torched Pete Warner's place left plenty of evidence that it wasn't an accident."

"I'm not surprised. The fire was supposed to be instructive. Some people who didn't get the picture before will get it now. It'll make Alberto's selling job easier."

"Maybe you can slip a mole into Alberto's operation. Get him from the inside."

"You read too many spy novels. Alberto keeps his cards close to his chest. His operation, as you call it, consists of him and his brother and Ben Krane. As far as I know, he doesn't even tell his wife or his other women anything about his business, and I doubt if Ben Krane wants to know any more than he has to, because he can never be held responsible for what he doesn't know. There's no way you can slip an informant into a circle as small as Alberto's."

"I don't read spy novels," I said. "Is Alberto doing business on other parts of the island, too?"

"I believe he's been seen in Vineyard Haven and West Tisbury."

"He must be a busy man."

"He's ambitious."

"Everybody's got a weakness. What's his?"

The chief thought for a moment, then said, "Women? A taste for the good life? Greed? He likes to take that boat of his out to the Dump to chase swordfish. That's why she's moored here right now instead of up in OB, by the way. Closer to the swordfishing grounds."

I had another thought. "Who does he care about? How about his mother?"

The chief shook his head. "He's living in a big house, she's living in the same dump she's always lived in. I don't think she's high on his list of things that are important."

"All right, how about his wife?"

"I don't think Alberto cares about anybody."

"Including Alexandro?"

"Including Alexandro. Alexandro is just another tool to Alberto. Alberto doesn't care about anything or anyone but himself."

It is a truism that if you can find out what a person values, you can get to that person. I remembered looking into Alberto's dead eyes and thought the chief was right about him. Alberto didn't care about anything or anybody. That made him the most dangerous kind of person there is.

I got up. "Well, thanks for the chat, Chief."

He stayed in his chair. "You stay out of this, J.W. You've already got yourself a busted wing for your trouble, and you're lucky it wasn't worse. You leave the Vegas boys to the authorities. Sooner or later they'll make a mistake and we'll nail them."

"Wise advice." And it was. But I didn't plan on taking it.

I got into the Land Cruiser and drove back to Oak Bluffs. The people in the Crandel house should have been up by now, and I wanted to talk to Cousin Buddy.

17

Fishermen were on the big bridge and out on the jetties on either side of the channel. All hoping for a big bass, I guessed, and none of them waiting for the Derby to start. A lot of whoppers had been caught there, and a lot more would be, since the bass were making a fine comeback after years of being pretty scarce in island waters.

The downside of this comeback was that as the bass were returning, the bluefish seemed to be getting rarer, giving rise once again to the theory that the fish came and went in alternate cycles. Since I was primarily a bluefish fisherman, this gave cause for pause. Would a time come when I would be obliged to hunt the elusive bass if I wanted to keep on fishing? It seemed possible.

I thought about Alberto Vegas being a fisherman. According to the chief, Alberto took the *Invictus* down to the Dump south of Noman's Land for swordfish. Did he fish the shoals and surf-cast for bass and bluefish, too? As a rule, the fisherpeople I knew were pretty friendly folk, but of course there were a few bad apples among them as there are in all groups. It was not too surprising that dead-eyed Alberto liked to wet a line.

Of course his work might interfere with his fishing. He seemed pretty busy with his business activities, spreading his interests out over the island as he was.

I thought of the ifs that had gotten me involved with him and his brother. If not for the ifs, I'd not know that the Vegas boys were even alive, but the ifs had intruded, and as they often do, they had changed everything. I'd now be doing something else if I didn't work for Stanley Crandel, if the faucet hadn't needed replacing, if I hadn't met Ivy and Julia, if there had been no California stalker, if Alexandro hadn't hated the two women on sight, if he hadn't showed up on the front lawn the next morning, and if I hadn't come out of the house at that moment. If, if, if. And there were, of course, earlier ifs: if the Vegas boys had had a decent father, if they hadn't gone to jail, if this, if that. A million ifs.

And now there would be more ifs, and it would only be much later that anyone would know their significance.

Off to my right, the waters of Nantucket Sound rolled across to the distant shore of Cape Cod, beautiful and indifferent to human cares. When I got to East Chop, the eastern light was flooding the front of the Crandel house, and the car belonging to the two Thornberry agents was in the driveway. I parked at the curb and went to the door and knocked. I could feel an eye at the peephole before the door opened. Jack Harley stepped back and I went in.

"I hear you have a new guest," I said.

"Word gets around. What the hell happened to you?"

Julia Crandel stuck her head out of the kitchen. "Oh, hi! Come and have some coffee. I want you to meet my cousin Buddy."

"Just the man I want to see," I said. She disappeared back into the kitchen.

I told Harley why I had my arm in a sling.

"Jesus," he said. "Alexandro Vegas?"

"I'm not sure, but he's on the top of my suspect list. You have any problems?"

"Pretty quiet. You've had problems enough for all of us."

"Yeah. Any news from the Coast?"

"Nobody's told me anything."

The closemouthed type. I went into the kitchen.

Ivy, Julia, and a young man were sitting at a table that held the remains of breakfast. The man was sleek and handsome, with coffee-colored skin and short, straight, black hair. He looked as though he spent time under a tanning machine, although that didn't seem to make much sense considering his heritage and that he lived in California, where he could get all the natural sun he might want.

"Buddy, this is Mr. Jackson," said Julia. "Mr. Jackson, this is my cousin Buddy Crandel. He just got in from Los Angeles. Goodness, what happened to you?"

"Call me J.W.," I said to Cousin Buddy, shaking his hand. He had dark, intelligent eyes and the firm grip of a man who did a lot of professional handshaking.

"And I'm just Buddy," he said, flashing a white smile. "Julia and Ivy have told me what a help you've been to them. I appreciate it."

"What happened to your arm? asked Julia with wide eyes.

"An accident. Nothing serious." It didn't seem the moment for true confessions, since I had no sense of Buddy Crandel's place in the scheme of things.

"Coffee?" asked Ivy, reaching for the pot. She seemed a bit edgy.

"Thanks. Black." I sat in a fourth chair and smiled at Buddy. "You just got in last night, I hear."

"Yes. Who told you?"

"It's a small island."

He put on a smile. "I guess I should know that. I've been coming here since I was a kid. Still . . ."

"My source isn't a secret. There are a lot of cops in town and they're keeping an eye on things. One of them told me you'd flown in. I'm glad you did. I tried to call you out there, but all I got was your machine."

"Well, here I am. When I found out these two were here by themselves and were being hassled, I came right out! It's maddening that they can't just be left alone!" His eyes flashed with an odd light.

"How'd you know they were being hassled?"

"I told him," said Julia, "when I phoned to tell him you wanted to talk with him."

"I didn't wait a second. I caught the first plane east."

I wondered who had appointed him their caretaker. He didn't look like the type who could stand up to real trouble, but you can never tell.

"Well, since you're here," I said, "I'd like to have you tell me what you can about that bad business out on the coast."

He spread his hands. "I'm afraid I can't help you. I don't know anything about it, really, except that it's scary."

"Sometimes people know things they don't know they know." I looked at the two women. "We can talk somewhere privately, if you'd prefer."

They exchanged quick glances, and Julia started to get up. But Ivy said, "No. I . . . we . . . want to hear whatever you say."

Julia opened her mouth, then closed it and sat back down.

I hesitated, then looked back at Buddy. "What I'm trying to find out is whether you know of anybody who might have had a reason to kill Dawn Dawson or might want to harm Ivy."

Ivy made a small wordless sound, and Buddy frowned. "What do you mean? Mackenzie Reed killed Dawn."

"But suppose he didn't? He says he didn't, and his lawyer says he didn't."

Buddy tilted his head. One of his hands held his coffee cup about halfway to his lips. He put the cup down. "The jury found him guilty. There was never any question about it. If anybody was ever guilty beyond a shadow of a doubt, it's Mackenzie Reed."

"Somebody is still sending letters to Ivy."

"I know! Somehow Reed is smuggling them out of prison! I don't know how, but it has to be him."

"Maybe. Probably, even. But suppose he isn't the killer. Suppose he's telling the truth about going into the apartment and finding Dawn Dawson already dead. If he didn't do it, it means that somebody else did. You were dating Dawn when it happened, and you dated Ivy before that, and you know a lot of the same people. You work in the movie business out there. Was there anyone you know who might have had it in for Dawn? Or for Ivy? Some of the people I've met in that racket can be pretty spiteful."

"The police asked me that, but I didn't know anybody who might have had a reason to hate Dawn or Ivy. Gossip runs like a river out there, and I think I'd have heard something if there was anything to hear. Besides, Dawn never mentioned any problems with anybody. She didn't have any enemies, and the only one Ivy had was that crazy Mackenzie Reed. And he's the one who did it!"

"How long did you date Ivy before you started dating Dawn Dawson?"

Buddy glanced at Ivy, who looked back at him with great, dark, enigmatic eyes.

He shrugged. "In California people date, then stop, then date other people. Ivy and I dated pretty seriously for a while, then we decided not to do that anymore. When we finally split up, it wasn't a big deal for either one of us, was it, Ivy?"

It was her turn to shrug. "No. You weren't the first guy I ever dated, and I wasn't your first girl."

"And there were no hard feelings," said Buddy with a nod. "Well, maybe a few, but nothing serious." He waved a hand. "Nothing we didn't get over pretty fast, anyway. And then Ivy started going out with other guys and I started dating Dawn." He smiled at Ivy. "And pretty soon we were friends again."

Her mouth smiled back. They were both very smooth, I thought.

"Wasn't it a little awkward when you started dating Dawn?" I asked, remembering some similar awkward situations I'd gotten myself into in my pre-Zee days. "I mean, she and Ivy were roommates."

He took his eyes away from Ivy's and turned them back to me. "Well, sure it was, but not for long. I'd met Dawn because she was Ivy's roommate, but we'd hit it off from the first. So it wasn't like I was somebody new on the scene when we started to date. Besides, Ivy was dating other guys by then, so it was like she was my sister more than an old girlfriend." He paused, as though deciding whether to go on, then said, "The police asked me a lot of questions about Dawn and me. I think they thought I might know something about her death. But of course I didn't."

"We usually get killed by people we know," I said. "Family, lovers, friends, people like that. That's why the cops were interested in you. If I'd been a cop out there, I would have been, too. But all they did was ask questions?"

"Yeah. Probably because they already had Mackenzie Reed with blood on his hands. Besides, I was up in San Francisco the day it happened, so they knew it couldn't be me. There was no way I could have slipped back to L.A. and killed her and then gone back north and never have been missed. I didn't know about it till the next day, when I got back to town." He shook his head, remembering. "Jesus! I couldn't believe it. I don't think I'll ever get over it."

Some people plan killings and alibis well ahead of the act, but most murders are spur-of-the-moment things that just happen. I thought the cops were probably right to take Buddy off their suspect list, but I left him on mine anyway. For the time being, at least.

"And now you're here," I said. "To make sure it doesn't happen again."

He made a fist with the hand that wasn't holding his coffee cup. "Yes! This man Vegas sounds like an animal! I won't let him hurt Ivy and Julia!"

"They have professional protection," I said.

"He didn't know that when he came," said Julia, putting a hand on his arm. "He thought we were alone."

Buddy's fist became a hand. He put it over hers and gave

her a wan smile. "I don't want anything to happen to my favorite cuz or my pal Ivy."

I left him and his pal and his favorite cuz and drove to the shop where my faxes were supposed to come in. They were there. I took them home and began to read them.

18

I read the newspaper stories first. They chronicled the sequence of events from the arrest of Mackenzie Reed to his imprisonment, and I learned not a whole lot more than I already knew, except from some sidebar and background stories that gave a bit more detail about the lifestyles of the young and beautiful and ambitious in Hollywood, including the participants in the murder drama. Fast living, casual and always shifting personal relationships, and unending efforts to achieve fame or at least work on the silver screen or television seemed to be the rule, and the associated passions, disappointments, and occasional triumphs were commonplace.

Dawn Dawson, Ivy Holiday, and Julia Crandel were but three more of the hundreds of aspiring actresses, and Ivy was rapidly becoming more than that, having made the most of a few small roles, having gained an award nomination for one of them, and then having achieved instant fame as a result of her strip act at the Academy Award ceremonies.

Buddy Crandel's aspirations were no less intense, though focused on offscreen work, and he was as much a part of the nightlife scene as were the three young women and their hundreds of fellow wanna-bes.

As I read the stories, I got the impression that if you wanted to survive in Hollywood, you had to be lucky and tough and probably both. Talent seemed to be less important, although it didn't hurt. Enduring personal ties and loyalties seemed rare. Rather, relationships flowered and faded fast and were readily sacrificed for the dream of stardom, if a choice was required. The person who was your greatest friend when you were down-and-out became a weight around your neck when you moved up, and your best pals up there on top left you if you slipped or fell from favor. Similarly, your eternal lover last month was often someone else's eternal lover this month.

Not that Hollywood was the only place such stuff happened. I was reminded of when I first took note of the Vineyard's winter inhabitants' inclination to marry, produce children, divorce, remarry, and produce more children, until, it seemed, everyone on the island was related to everyone else.

When I finished with the newspaper stories, I read the trial transcripts. Most of what I learned was familiar to me. Mackenzie Reed had been fixated on Ivy for months, had written her letters, followed her, tried to get close to her, phoned her, and otherwise intruded upon her life to such a degree that she had gotten an unlisted phone number, had left her apartment and moved in with Dawn Dawson, and, finally, had gotten a restraining order against him. All three actions were to no avail, since he soon knew both her new number and her address and was once again following her.

The morning of the killing, Ivy had gone to work, leaving by a back door that led to the parking area where she kept her car, and Dawn was home alone. Reed had found the front door unlocked and had gone in. There, with a steak knife taken from the kitchen of the apartment, he had stabbed Dawn Dawson a dozen times. He then had panicked and run out into the street, his hands and clothes bloody, where he was immediately arrested by police officers who were passing by in their cruiser.

The evidence against him was overwhelming: Dawn Dawson's body was still warm; his prints were on the knife; the blood on his hands and clothes was hers; his letters to Ivy were filled with statements about his frustration when he saw her with other men, and the meaninglessness of his life without her, and with graphic descriptions of the sexual acts they would perform when she finally agreed to love him as much as he loved her.

With nothing to lose by putting his client on the witness stand, the flamboyant William Peterson Calhoun, the best lawyer Reed's father's money could buy, had done that, and Mackenzie Reed had told his tale, which was the predictable one that he had found Dawn Dawson dead, had touched the fatal knife, had gotten her blood on his hands and clothes as he had attempted to discover if she was still alive, had panicked when he realized that he would be accused of killing her, and had tried to run away, which he realized now was a foolish mistake that only made things worse for him.

The jury had taken little time to find him guilty, and I guessed that had I been a member of that jury, it wouldn't have taken me long, either.

Some details were new to me, but nothing surprising. Other fingerprints were at the murder scene, but only the ones you would expect: those of Ivy, who lived there, of Buddy Crandel, who was dating Dawn, and those of the landlord and friends of Ivy's and Dawn's. Although the police were confident that they had their killer, they had interviewed everyone whose prints had been found at the scene and had eliminated them all as suspects.

One oddity was that the knife had only Mackenzie Reed's fingerprints on it, whereas, since it was one of the apartment's kitchen utensils, presumably the prints of one or both of the girls should also have been on it. Calhoun had made as much of this as he could, suggesting that it clearly showed that the real murderer had wiped the knife clean before fleeing the scene. But the prosecutor had a simpler explanation: Mackenzie Reed himself had wiped the knife clean, but had then inadvertently touched it again before fleeing.

I thought back to the few murder scenes I'd observed while on the Boston PD and realized once again that Dostoyevsky had been right about killers: most of them are pretty ordinary people who are not overly smart, and even the brightest of them often make stupid mistakes. The killers who get away with it usually do so because they're just lucky or because most police, like most killers, are also pretty ordinary people and not overly smart and make stupid mistakes.

When I finished the transcripts, I discovered that I had copies of some official police reports on the Dawson case, the Freed case, and the Hawkins case. Son of a gun! How had Peter Brown gotten his hands on them? My opinion of Western Security Services went right up.

The reports were not, of course, high-class literature, being written, as they usually are, by cops who never majored in English. Police reports can be funny, in fact, even when they attempt to deal seriously with horrendous crimes. But I wasn't interested in the literary quality of these reports; I was interested in what the cops had seen and heard.

They had talked to a lot of people and hadn't found any reason to think that anyone but Mackenzie Reed had killed Dawn Dawson. They had discovered love affairs and hard feelings and drug use and other illegalities, mostly minor, but nothing having anything to do with the murder. I was interested to learn a bit more about the players I knew:

Buddy Crandel, for instance, was something of a swordsman and hadn't always left his maidens laughing when he moved on to his next conquest. There were feelings of anger and betrayal in his wake, and no one had been surprised when he had dropped Ivy and picked up Dawn Dawson. Similarly, no one had expected his affair with Dawn to last long.

Ivy Holiday, no virgin herself, but not given to one-night stands, either, was known for her temper and iron will as well as for her talent and did not take lightly being denigrated as a woman, especially a black woman, or being told how to live her private life. The Academy Award stunt was apparently quite in character. In fact, Ivy had once gotten so angry at a rival starlet that she had thrown her through a brick wall, which, fortunately for the starlet, had only been a painted prop and not the real thing.

Dawn Dawson's private reputation had been at odds with her appearance and public persona, which had been that of the sweet girl next door. She had been, apparently, one of the more serious party girls in town and had a trail of lovers, each one of whom the police had been obliged to track down just in case one of them had decided to do her in for old times' sake. None had. It was rumored, as well, that she had frequented the casting couch and habitually used illegal chemical additives to stay perky. On the other hand, she had been thought of as kind and generous, and as a "good kid" in spite of her tendency to bed-hop a bit more than most.

Julia Crandel was a different breed of cat. She already knew she could act because she had done it on the stage in New York, and so she didn't need to hang around with wanna-bes for moral support. But she did need to find acting jobs and to keep eating in the meantime. Too proud to support her acting habit on her share of a Crandel trust fund, she got a part-time day job in a grocery store, where she could get food cheap at the end of the day, and avoided partying at night so her money would last longer. Her agent had gotten her some roles in TV commercials, and she was taking acting classes while she sought a start in film.

Like a lot of Crandels, she was smart and focused, friendly and well-liked, but she was also sufficiently uneasy about herself and her life to want a therapist. Thus her relationship with Dr. Jane Freed, who was the second murder victim in Ivy Holiday's life.

Julia was, in fact, a central figure in Ivy's drama. They had met through Julia's cousin Buddy, and Julia had later met Dawn through Dawn's friendship with Ivy. Ivy had become Jane Freed's patient at Julia's suggestion, and after Dawn's death, Julia had become Ivy's roommate. They were living together at the time that Dick Hawkins had been run down in the street outside their apartment building.

It occurred to me that since Ivy would never have known either Dr. Freed or Dick Hawkins if it weren't for Julia, and if, as Julia seemed to suspect, their deaths were somehow linked to Ivy, it could be argued that Julia was in part responsible for those deaths. The ifs, again. If this hadn't happened, this other thing wouldn't have happened. If, if, if.

Madness.

The reports on the Freed case told me little more than I already knew. Along with her paying clients, the doctor, being persuaded that she had a duty to the poor and destitute, had donated a few hours a week to people who were down-and-out or otherwise unable to afford private psychiatric service. She also kept a small supply of drugs, mostly sedatives, in her office.

Whoever killed her had not broken in, suggesting that the killer and Dr. Freed might have known each other. The doctor had been killed by blows to the head. The killer had used a paperweight from her desk and had afterward rifled the medicine cabinet and the file cabinets. The police theorized that the motive for the crime was the killer's desire for drugs, but were fuzzier about why the file cabinets were also in disarray. Their guesses were, one, that the killer might have hoped to find more drugs there; and two, that the killer, presuming that the police would suspect one of the doctor's patients of having committed the crime, might have taken his or her file out of the cabinet so as to remove his or her name from the list of suspects.

However, a list of the patients' names was later found in a separate file, and all of those patients' files were still in the office, indicating that stealing a file hadn't been a motive after all.

A lot of patients had been questioned, but nothing had

come of the work. The case was still open and the investigation was still going on when anyone had time to devote to it.

Ditto for the Hawkins case. Hawkins had been run down as he tried to stop the theft of his own car in front of his own apartment house. After the hit-and-run, the car had been found in a parking lot not too far away. There were no prints and no one had seen anything conclusive or even helpful. The driver could have been either a man or a woman, according to the only witness, an elderly lady walking her dog.

Hawkins was the grandfatherly type who liked women. He rented his apartments to them, protected them and cared for them, and hovered over them closer than some of them liked. Had he been younger, more of the women who rented from him might have told him to mind his own business, but he was an old guy, so most of them put up with him, and only a few moved out or told him to keep away from them.

I wondered if some boyfriend or ex-husband of one of the women had run him down out of spite or anger or jealousy. Or had one of the women in his building done it to keep him away from her? Or had it just been an accident: speeding car thief hits car owner while making getaway?

The police had wondered the same things and had rounded up the usual suspects and asked the usual questions. As far as I could tell, they were still asking them and hoping for a break in the case.

The last faxes were copies of a couple of Mackenzie Reed's letters to Ivy before the killing, and of a couple received after Reed was in prison. They were typed on different machines, but they were of a kind, speaking of the same longings, describing the same desolation of spirit, and giving the same graphic descriptions of the sex he and Ivy would enjoy when at last she was his. Ivy had reason to be nervous.

I thought about that, then read the letters again, and then again. Spooky stuff.

It was noon. I got out a Sam Adams and made myself a sandwich out of homemade white bread and cold bluefish fillet, left over from stuffed bluefish I'd cooked a few days earlier.

Delish!

I thought about everything I'd read, and about everything that had happened since Ivy and Julia had arrived on the island. Back in my brain somewhere a little computer was clicking and humming, but it was a Jurassic machine and hopelessly slow. I left it to its work and drove back to Oak Bluffs.

The only thing I was pretty sure of was that Julia was financing me and Thornberry Security out of her trust fund. She sure wasn't doing it out of her earnings as a grocery clerk or an actress.

19

First I went back and had another look at Alexandro's house. It was on the dead-end loop of a road in an expensive development off County Road. Neither the house nor grounds looked any better cared for than when I'd last seen them, but I hadn't come by to do an assessment of Alexandro's lifestyle. I looped the loop once and drove away, after noting the forest in back and on both sides of the house, pretty much isolating it from his nearest neighbor, who lived several hundred yards away. The neighbor's place, like others along the road, but unlike Alexandro's, was neat and polished looking, and I suspected that the owners hoped that slovenly Alexandro would soon sell to someone who would be more inclined to keep up the place.

Not many people seemed to be home, which wasn't too surprising since a lot of the houses were summer places, and the year-rounders' kids would be in school while mom or dad or both were probably working. Parked in front of one house was a guy sitting in a car reading a newspaper. I thought it looked like the *Vineyard Gazette,* and I thought the guy looked a lot like a West Tisbury cop I'd seen around. He looked at me as I drove in and again as I drove out.

When I got back out near County Road, I pulled off to the side and parked and got out a map. The forest behind Alexandro's house reached back quite a distance before it touched the road of another development off Barnes Way. I imagined that if Alexandro was so inclined, he could probably sit on his rear porch and see an occasional deer go by. A lot of deer were on the island, and they probably liked the woods back there.

I wondered who had moved the curtain in Alexandro's house the first time I'd seen it. His wife? A child? A girl-friend?

Could be. When I was first a cop, it had surprised me to learn just how many terrible people had homes and fami-lies and friends in spite of meriting love from no one. There were women who loved brutes, and men who loved vicious women, and many such couples produced children who were traumatized from birth but loved their parents in spite of beatings and unspeakable abuse. Alexandro was the product of such a home, as were most of the truly vio-lent people I had met. The surprising thing was not that such people were produced by such histories, but that so many people overcame such childhoods and became nor-mal citizens.

Which gave rise to the eternal nature-nurture question: Are we born with sealed fates, or do our situations deter-mine those fates?

I chose a third option, holding that in spite of all evi-dence to the contrary, we can choose how we shall act and are, therefore, responsible for those acts. And that it was particularly important to be responsible in a universe with-out moral form, where there was no God to establish and uphold ethical law.

Ivan Karamazof would, of course, disagree.

Such erudition.

I put the map away and drove to Alberto's house. Not far from his house, pulled off beside Barnes Road, there was another car with another man in it. We looked at each other as I drove by. Another up-island cop. Alberto's house on the bluff overlooking Lagoon Pond was a big, modern place, complete with two-car garage, large front lawn, and a little barn to one side where Alberto could keep his tools and toys. Behind the house, a drive led down toward the dock and boathouse. I parked in the driveway and knocked on the door with the brass knocker shaped like a scallop shell.

Nothing happened. Mrs. Alberto was, of course, at the office, and Mr. Alberto was no doubt out on the road drumming up business. I drove back to the cop in the car and stopped across the road. He eyed me warily. I got out and went over to him. He rolled down his window.

"Where's Alberto?" I asked.

He studied me. "Do I know you?"

"J. W. Jackson. Alberto's not home. Do you know where he went?"

"I'm afraid I can't help you, mister."

I dug around in my brain and came up with a name. "You're Fred Sierra. You're with the Chilmark PD."

"I'm off duty. Sorry I can't help you." He started to roll up the window.

I pointed at my sling. "I think Alexandro did this, and I want to talk to Alberto about it."

"Oh, yeah. I heard about you. How you doing?"

"I'm okay. Luckier than Larry Curtis, anyway. You know where I can find Alberto?"

"You should probably leave this to the police."

"I don't plan on shooting anybody. I just want to talk to Alberto."

"What about?"

"His little brother's wild ways. I want Alberto to rein him in."

"Ha! Fat chance of that! Alexandro's his muscle."

"I'll reason with him."

Sierra gave a little snort. "Sure."

"I saw one of you guys over near Alexandro's place. There are a lot of you around. If you keep the Vegas boys under a microscope, maybe you'll slow them down. Not even Alexandro is going to burn down somebody's place or break their bones with a tire iron if there are a bunch of cops watching his every move."

"Actually, I'd kind of like to have him try, just so I could throw his ass in jail."

I drove into Oak Bluffs and found a parking place on Circuit Avenue without any problems. I can even do that in the summer, sometimes, but rarely as easily because more people come to the Vineyard every year.

Vineyarders constantly fuss about the increasing numbers. The merchants and hotel keepers need the money they bring, but on the other hand if you're not a merchant or somebody else living off tourists, you want to be the last person off the ferry. It's an old problem for resort areas everywhere: you need visitors, but if you get too many, you begin to destroy the very charms that the visitors come to enjoy. No islanders wanted the Vineyard to become a mini–Cape Cod, but nobody seemed to know how to keep it from happening.

Neither did I.

I also didn't want it to be controlled by Alberto Vegas or anybody like him. I couldn't do much about the tourist problem, but maybe I could do something about Alberto. I walked upstairs to his office. Sylvia Vegas, still sporting a puffy face and still reading her romance novel or one that looked a lot like it, stared at me from behind her desk.

"You remember me? John Appleseed? I was in here just a while back."

She was chewing gum. Her jaws worked while she studied me. "You're a liar," she finally said. "Your name ain't Appleseed. It's Jackson."

"Gosh. You got me. I admit it." I looked around the room. It was empty. I looked back at her. "I want to talk to your hubby. You know where he is?"

"You got one arm busted already. You must be trying for two."

I examined my sling. "Did your husband do this? Is that what you're saying, Mrs. Vegas?"

She put her book aside. "I don't know what you're talking about."

"Because if he did, maybe you should talk with the police before he gets into more trouble."

"A wife don't have to testify against her husband."

"You might not have to, but you might want to."

She frowned. "Why would I want to do that?"

"To keep from being an accessory after the fact, maybe? I think you should talk with your lawyer. Ben Krane, isn't it?"

She eyed me from under heavy lids. "Get out of here, or I'll call the cops."

I went to a window and looked down onto Circuit Avenue. "You won't have to call very loud. They're watching everything you people do, just hoping one of you will make a mistake and they can throw the whole bunch of you in jail where you belong. Take a peek. I think one of Oak Bluffs' finest is right across the street there, looking up this way."

"Get out of here."

"Where's Alberto?"

"How the hell should I know?"

I reached across and picked up her novel. It looked like the same cover I'd seen before, but I couldn't be sure. The woman's breasts and the man's muscles looked about the same size, at any rate, and their faces had the same bored look. "I'm in no rush. You won't mind if I read this while I wait. I'll answer the phone if you want to go up the street and get yourself another one."

I put a chair against a wall and sat down.

"You'd better get out of here while you can still walk."

"I'll wait." Then I added what I hoped was a useful lie: "Several cops know I'm here, so I doubt if Alberto will want to work me over and throw me out the window or anything like that."

She glared at me, but said nothing.

I began to read the book. It wasn't bad. A beautiful, passionate young woman, traveling by sea to meet an older, rich, aristocratic husband-to-be to make a marriage that would save her father from financial problems brought about by evildoers, is taken captive by a bold, handsome pirate who lusts after her lovely bod and who, in spite of his lordly buccaneer airs, makes her heart beat faster.

I was pretty sure that I'd seen similar stories on late-night TV, staring Errol Flynn and Maureen O'Hara or Paul Henreid and some other fair damsel. No matter. It was a story always worth the telling, even though I knew from the first that the husband-to-be would turn out to be the very villain who had ruined the young woman's father and that the pirate would turn out to be another of his victims who, in fact, was the legitimate heir of the fortune the wicked duke controlled and that everything was going to turn out well in the end, although not without considerable danger and near heartbreak.

We don't read such stories or watch such movies so we'll be surprised; we do it so we won't be surprised. The seven-foot shelf of trash literature holds our favorite books. The leather-bound classics are rarely opened.

I had just gotten to the part where the woman daringly seizes a dagger to defend her virtue against the apparently forthcoming ravages of the manly pirate, when the door of the office opened and Alberto Vegas came in.

He looked at me and then at his wife and then at me again, wondering where he had seen me.

"It's that Jackson guy who said he was Appleseed," said his wife, pointing at me. "He's been here an hour. He won't leave."

"He won't, eh?" said Vegas, eyeing me. "I seen you someplace. Oh, yeah. Down at the docks in Edgartown. You got something to say before I kick your sorry ass downstairs?"

"Maybe you can kick it and maybe you can't," I said, closing the book and dropping it on the floor.

Someone else followed him into the office. A refrigerator, or maybe a small tank. Alexandro. He stared at me. If there was going to be any kicking done, I was now pretty sure who would be doing it. It wouldn't be me.

— 20 —

I felt as if I were in a cage with two angry hippopotami, but tried not to show it.

"You've got a problem," I said to Alberto, acutely aware that a psychiatrist might call the phrase a classic case of transference.

Alberto, unaware of the clichés bandied about in Psych 101, looked at me through narrowed eyes. "No. You've got a problem. You come in here telling lies about who you are, then you bad-mouth me to Eddie Francis, and now you won't leave my office when my wife asks you to. Alex, throw this bum out."

Sylvia's voice had a warning note in it. "He says the cops know he's up here, Al. He says they're watching the place."

But Alexandro only smiled. "So what? I think he's gonna fall downstairs." He started for me.

I pointed a finger at the oncoming train. I also stayed right in the chair, in part because there was nowhere else to go. Seeing myself tumbling down the stairs, bones splintering, I said, "Your brother is your problem, Alberto. You have a pretty good thing going, but Alexandro, here, is fucking it up for you. He's all muscle and no brain. I heard you were smart. I guess I heard wrong."

Alexandro got to me and grabbed my collar. With his other hand, he swatted my bad arm. A bolt of pain shot through me. He grinned and yanked me up as though I weighed nothing. "So long, girly girl. Accident time for you." He jerked me toward the door.

"Hold it, Alex," said Alberto.

Alexandro kept going.

"I said hold it," said Alberto, stepping in front of him.

Alberto was about six-five and weighed around 250, all of it muscle, but he was small compared with Alexandro, who was pro lineman size. Still, when Alberto put up his hand, Alexandro stopped.

"Let go of him, Alex," said Alberto.

Alexandro hesitated, then gave me a push. I went backward and almost fell. "Fuck you, girly girl. I ain't through with you yet, you fucker."

My left arm hurt so much that the world was gray. I leaned against the wall, weak and sick, and tried to will the pain away.

Alberto nodded toward the door. "You get out of here, Jackson. Right now, on your own. You don't go, I'll give you back to Alex."

"I came up here to talk to you. If you're smart, you'll listen."

Alberto studied me with his empty, wily, animal eyes. He had no aura that I could see. Some people believe that if you have no aura, you have no soul.

"All right. You want to talk, talk. I don't like what you say, then you go back to Alex. And cops or no cops, we got three witnesses to say that after you left here, you must have fainted because of that arm of yours and fell downstairs and killed yourself."

"You've been hanging around your little brother too long. You're beginning to think like he does. You're dumbing down, Alberto."

"You're using up what little time you got," said Alberto.

"You sure you want to talk in front of these two? You let people like these know everything you know, pretty soon you may not be the boss any longer. You'll have a committee."

Perhaps he frowned just a little, but all Alberto said was "You got about thirty seconds. You use them any way you want."

I shrugged. "Have it your way." I leaned on the wall and gently rubbed my bad arm. "Like I said, you've got yourself a pretty good thing going for you. Protection racket, but disguised as a legit operation, complete with written contracts and everything. Hell, it's not much different than a legit business fraternity asking members to join up for the common good. Hard for the cops to nail you, if everybody stays happy, and so far nobody has complained. Not too much, at least. And business is good.

"But everybody's not going to be happy much longer." I jabbed a thumb in Alexandro's direction. "Because you got yourself a loose cannon. It was probably okay when little Alex, here, was still in line, doing what he was told. Torching a place here and there, beating somebody up in some alley, stuff like that, but always for the good of the company. You know what I mean? But now Alex is doing other stuff on his own, and he's attracting a lot of attention that isn't going to do your business any good."

I figured my thirty seconds were about up, but Alberto wasn't looking at his watch. He was looking at me. I took that as a good sign.

"Think about it," I said. "Actually, I imagine you've already thought about it. Alexandro broke into the Crandels' house and tried to rape the women in there. I don't think you told him to do that as part of company policy, since all it did was draw attention to him and, indirectly, to you. I think he did it all by himself because he's a racist pig and a woman hater who can't control himself. And then he nearly killed that young cop. Maybe you told him to, and maybe you didn't, but in any case it was a stupid move because cops take care of their own and now you've got every one on the island and some from off-island on your case, watching every move you make, checking every document Enterprise Management has ever filed, just waiting for you to make the mistake you're sure as hell going to make as long as Alexandro, here, is out there causing trouble for you." I paused.

"And then there's me," I said. "Little Alex there, with the bean for a brain, decided to take me out with a crowbar. And for what? I was only a bit player who probably never would have gotten more involved if he hadn't tried to kill me like he tried to kill Larry Curtis. But now I am involved, thanks to him. And I'm no easy mark. I popped a cap or two that night, and if I get harried, I may pop some more, only this time I'll be looking at what's in front of me. If you told him to try to kack me, I'm wasting my time talking to you because you're just as stupid as he is. But if he did it by himself, just for laughs because he's a psycho punk, then maybe you should think about reining him in before he sinks you and your whole damned ship. You don't need the enemies he'll bring to you."

I looked at Alexandro. "You're a complete fool, Alex. You're stupid and psychotic at the same time. What little sense you might have had as a kid got fucked out of you up there in Cedar Junction. All you are now is an ape with a sore asshole." I looked back at Alberto. "Watch. You'll see what I mean."

And I was right. Alexandro gave a roar and leaped toward me. I slipped to the right as Alberto shouted, "Hold it, Alex!" and stepped between us. But Alexandro came right on. It was linebacker against lineman, and they met with a crash. I ducked around them and got to the door as the room seemed to rock and roll.

"You control him, Alberto!" I shouted. "Or he'll ruin you!"

Alexandro and Alberto wrestled and filled the air with invectives, and I turned and hurried downstairs and out into the street.

I didn't know how long Alberto could hold Alexandro back, so I walked quickly down the street to the Land Cruiser and got inside. From there I could see the door at the foot of the stairs. I wondered who would come out first. I wondered if one of them would kill the other upstairs. It was Alberto's will against Alexandro's muscles, and I didn't know who would win if they went all the way to the wall.

I waited awhile, but no one showed. Then, thinking that I had given Alberto enough to brood about, I drove to the police station and went in to see Lisa Goldman. Dominic Agganis and a cop from Vineyard Haven were with her in the office. Since I had no secrets, I told them what had happened.

"Oh, very bright," said Dom. "Now you've really made them mad. Up to now, they were probably only annoyed, but now they're pissed to a fare-thee-well."

"So what?" I asked. "What are they going to do that they weren't going to do anyway?"

"How about break the rest of your bones?"

"I can take care of myself."

Dom shook his head. "Sure you can. You did a great job protecting your arm."

"And what about Zee and your kids?" said Lisa. "Can you take care of them, too?"

"Yes."

She looked at me.

"No," I said. "I'm not sure. But right now they're all over on the mainland, so they're okay."

"But they'll be back sometime."

True. Had I made things better or worse? If Alexandro had been angry before, he was a lot angrier now, and if I was right about him, he was apt to go off the deep end and do God knew what. That was bad. But it was possible that I'd gotten Alberto to put a noose on him and hold him back so he wouldn't do anything else to imperil Alberto's grand plans. A loose cannon like Alexandro could be more trouble than he was worth in an organization such as Alberto apparently had in mind.

I offered this theory to Lisa and Agganis. Neither of them seemed impressed by it.

"They're brothers," said Dom. "They ain't kissing kin, but they've been together all their lives. They even went to the pen together. They're close. Alberto isn't going to break with Alexandro."

"Not even if it costs him his protection racket?"

Lisa's elbows were on her desk. She put her hands together, fingertip to fingertip, thumb to thumb, and looked at me with her intelligent cop's eyes.

"It hasn't cost him yet, and maybe it won't. But Dom is right. You've made yourself some real enemies this time. Up to now, you were just a nuisance. Now you've made it personal. You be very careful, because you're right about Alexandro. He's a psycho case."

"I plan to be careful."

She nodded. "Good. And there's another thing."

"What?"

"Alexandro might deserve killing, but he's got the same rights as anybody else. If anything happens to him, you'd better be sure that you're innocent as a lamb, because you'll be high on the suspect list."

I had been expecting just such a warning. "Have you heard me threaten him?"

"No."

"Or anybody else?"

"No."

"Have I ever killed anybody?"

"I know you still carry a bullet from a perp you shot when you were on the Boston PD, but that happened in the line of duty. You never killed anybody else that I know of."

"That shooting was one reason I hung up my badge. I don't plan on killing anybody else."

"Okay, J.W. As long as we're clear about this. You leave the Vegas brothers to the police. They're our job."

"And welcome to it. How's Larry Curtis?"

"He's alive."

I remembered Curtis's face. He was a good-looking lad. He hadn't deserved what had happened to him. Or maybe I was wrong. Maybe we all deserve what happens to us.

I went out of the police station and drove to East Chop.

21

Jack Harley opened the door of the Crandel house. He eyed me with neither rancor nor affection.

"Nobody home but us chickens," he said. "Everybody else has gone to the beach. Place they call the Inkspot or some such thing. Is that a racist name, or what?"

"You can probably get an argument about that, but you won't get it from me." I felt a frown on my face. "I don't know if it's smart for you guys to split up like this."

Harley didn't share my concern. "Well, smart or not, the rest of them are at that beach and I'm the housekeeper today, just in case the house needs keeping."

"Keep it carefully, then. Alexandro Vegas is in a very bad mood and just might decide to take it out on you if he comes this way."

"I get paid to handle guys like him," said Harley in a tough-guy voice.

Spoken like someone who'd never seen Alexandro. Even as I was being irked by his naïveté, I was pretty sure I'd said things just as dumb.

"I hope it's a good salary," I said, "and that the deal includes insurance."

Then he gave a little smile. "Don't worry. I was a track-man. He can chase me, but he won't catch me. And if he does, I have six friends who'll help me out."

I felt instantly better about him. "You're dressed."

He patted his hip. "Part of the uniform."

"Good. But don't let him get too close to you. He's very quick."

"I'll keep distance between us."

A good idea. Every year cops get killed, sometimes with their own pistols, and usually at close quarters: in doorways, in small rooms, in cars. In fact, I'd once read a study of cops fatally shot while on duty that indicated that none of them had been killed at distances over twenty feet. The best protection against being shot to death was the same as that for avoiding pregnancy: several yards of air between participating parties.

I got back into the Land Cruiser and drove to Sea View Avenue, where I parked and walked down onto the part of the beach that's known as the Inkwell, because of its popularity with the locals of African descent. I'd been told that the people who frequented the spot had given the location its name, so it was up to linguists and social commentators, and not to me, to decide whether it was a racist term.

In the summer, the Oak Bluff beaches are full of sound and bright colors, as visitors and home owners alike loll under beach umbrellas or sop up sun and surf and suds in air filled with laughter, shouts, and the music from boom boxes. Although it's a convivial place and seems to suit OBers just fine, it's too crowded and noisy for Zee and me, so when we want a beach, we drive out to the far shores of Chappaquiddick, where we can be alone with the sand and sea.

Now, in September, most of the summer people had gone back to America, and it wasn't hard to spot Mills, Ivy Holiday, and the cousins. The last three were stretched on bright beach towels, were clothed in minimal, bikini-style bathing suits that revealed more than they concealed, and were shiny with tanning lotion, as they lay in the early-fall sun. They were an eye-grabbing trio, without a doubt, and I ogled Ivy and Julia appreciatively as I approached.

Is there anything more appealing to the eye than a beautiful woman? Well, maybe; Zee would no doubt argue that a hunky man was more interesting, and there were those who favored members of their own gender. But I was male and heterosexual and had no doubt at all about where beauty lay. Right now, it lay on two towels on Inkwell beach.

Mills wasn't in the running for the glamour title. He was sitting in an aluminum beach chair, wearing regular clothing, sans shoes, which were hung around his neck as a concession to the soft, yellow sand. He, too, would be armed, I figured and was glad. As I came up, he watched me.

"What's up?" he asked, and his voice roused the others, who rolled their heads toward me, then sat up.

"Just reporting in," I said.

"Hi, J.W.," said Julia. "How's your arm? You never said how you hurt it. I hope it's better."

I squatted on my heels. To my left, the blue waters of the sound reached toward Cape Cod, and overhead the lighter blue of the sky curved down to the eastern horizon. The bluffs cut off the southwestern wind, so it was warm and summerlike there on the beach, and there was no hint of Elmer even occupying the same earth. What had the weather been like when Cain killed Abel, or David had done in Goliath? Had the days been as fair and beautiful as this one? Or had the winds been raging and the rain blowing flat and cold, and the oceans roaring?

"The bone is cracked. Nothing serious, I'm told." Then I looked at Ivy. "But I think I should bring you up-to-date."

"That sounds pretty heavy," said Ivy, who looked like an ebony naiad.

"You can decide how heavy it is." I told them about how I'd been attacked and what had just happened in Alberto Vegas's office. When I was done, I said, "Alexandro is in a bad mood, so I think you should all be especially careful, just in case you bump into each other." I offered them my view that they should stick together for safety.

"That'll be the day," said Ivy. "No man is going to keep me from doing what I want to do!"

Buddy Crandel's face was angry. "You've made a fine mess of things! Goading those men like that! My God! Are you *trying* to cause trouble?"

Ivy looked at him, then at Julia. I could barely see her eyes behind her dark glasses.

"You're not the only people who have trouble," I said to Buddy. "I have it, too. The Vegas brothers are trouble for a lot of people. We all have to be careful."

"But you've made it worse!"

"You may be right." I stood up. "It's spilled beans, in any case. Just be careful. I don't think Alexandro is too stable."

Buddy was on his feet. "I think it would be best if you just get out of our lives, Jackson. You're more trouble than good." He looked at Julia. "You hired him. Fire him before he does more damage. I'm here, and Mills and Harley are professionals. We don't need Jackson."

Ivy was studying me. "Maybe you're right," she said. "Is he right, Mr. Jackson?"

"You have two problems," I said. "One is Alexandro Vegas, and the other is the stalker who seems to be trailing you around. I really didn't get hired to take care of Alexandro, I got hired to try to track down the stalker. I'll be glad to give back Julia's money anytime she wants. But as long as I keep the money, I'm also going to keep my nose in this mess."

"And if Julia fires you, are you going to take your nose out?"

I heard a siren somewhere on the far side of town. Someone else with troubles and someone else trying to help out. Trouble is sure, but often succor follows. "If you fire me," I said to Julia, "I won't owe you anything one way or the other. I'll do as I please."

A little smile played on her lips. "You do as you please anyway, it seems to me, whether I pay you or not. I can keep my money and still get the same results."

"Maybe it'll work out like that. Maybe not."

She made up her mind. "Stay on the job a little longer. That way I'll at least get reports about what you're up to."

"You're making a mistake," Buddy said to her.

"It won't be the first one I've made," said Julia, lying back down on her beach towel.

I looked at Mills. "Keep in touch. And be careful."

"Sure."

Sure. I walked away, feeling the sand grab at my feet as I went.

I drove through Oak Bluffs and went out along Newton Avenue. I approached the still smoldering ruin of Pete Warner's house and could smell the sour odor of smoke as I passed. An ambulance was coming up the driveway toward the road. Now I knew why I'd heard the siren. I pulled over and watched it go by me, headed for the hospital. A fire truck was still down by the blackened remains of the house, and a couple of firemen were hosing down a pile of rubble that was still smoking. I drove down and got out. The firemen looked tired.

"Where's Pete?" I asked.

"Hospital."

My heart beat a bit faster. "I just saw the ambulance. That him?"

"His wife collapsed. They just took her out of here. Pete's riding with her." The fireman tapped his chest. "Too much for her. Bad ticker, I guess. We kept her breathing." He shrugged. "Not good, though."

"I'll get out of your way."

If Pete's wife died, Alexandro would have taken another step down his steep road. As far as I knew, he'd done a lot of damage to people and property, but up to now he hadn't succeeded in killing anybody. I wondered if it would make any difference to him if she died and guessed that it wouldn't. He struck me as one of those people who never figure that they've done anything wrong. They go to their graves thinking their victims deserved what happened to them because we're all animals in a jungle, and that the law of the jungle is that the strong shall devour the weak, and you only get to possess something—life, property, whatever—as long as you're strong enough to defend it. When a stronger animal comes by and takes it away from you, it becomes his for as long as he wants it or can hold it against the next predator.

It is a popular theory among the criminal and the powerful classes, and what is called civilized behavior is a thin shield against it.

I drove back to Barnes Road and went on until I came to the newish dirt roads leading off to the left. I took the one that I remembered from my map reading. It led past houses on either side until it made a turn and headed off at a ninety-degree angle. I turned the corner and was pleased to see a summer house sitting amid the trees on the right. The grass was long and there was that feeling of disuse about the place that empty houses have. Better yet, there wasn't another house in view.

I parked in the driveway and knocked on the front door, just in case I was wrong about the owners of the place having gone away for the winter. But I knew I wasn't wrong. I take care of several houses during the off-season, and I know what they feel like. I got back into the Land Cruiser and drove around to the back of the house, where I parked out of sight of the road.

There, I got out the map again and studied it. I was about a half mile from the back of Alexandro's house. I got out of the car and walked through the trees and underbrush until I could see the house ahead of me. I scouted to the left and to the right, just in case some house was nearby that I hadn't noticed when I'd driven by earlier.

When I was sure that there wasn't, I eased closer to Alexandro's place and studied it from the deep shadow of a large oak.

The house was as disreputable from behind as it was from in front. An expensive-looking but rusting barbecue grill and a round plastic table with an umbrella opened over it were in the backyard. Plastic lawn chairs were here and there, one or two with broken legs and others lying on their sides. Beside a heavy wooden lawn chair was a wooden table with a large ceramic ashtray on it. Alexandro's chair, for sure, since no plastic chair would hold his weight. Beer bottles were scattered on the lawn, and a plastic rubbish barrel overflowed by the corner of the house.

As I looked, the back door opened and a woman came out. She had a beer bottle in one hand and a cigarette in the other. She sat down by the table and looked right at me.

22

She wasn't seeing anything, she was just staring. I didn't move, and after a bit her eyes wandered off in another direction, while she sipped her beer and drew on her cigarette.

She was a youngish woman whose brown hair was loosely tied back in a ponytail. She wore a flannel shirt, jeans, and bedroom slippers. Her face was free of makeup. A bruise was on her forehead and others were on her arms.

Alexandro's wife? His girlfriend? The face behind the window shade?

She had a look of carelessness about her, as though neither what she did nor how she appeared mattered to her or to anyone else.

I wondered, as many have, why women stay with men who beat them. None of the answers—fear, love, economic dependence, self-loathing, and the others—gave me any satisfaction.

No toys or playthings were in the yard, and I decided that meant no children were in the house, since otherwise, things being as they were in Alexandro's yard, their gear would have been as abandoned and scattered about as everything else was.

After a while, the woman tossed the butt of her cigarette one way and the empty bottle the other and went into the house. The door slammed behind her.

I studied the place a little longer, then moved through the trees first to one side, then back around to the other, and studied it some more, taking in the locations of the windows, the rear entrance to the basement, and, of course, the rear door.

I wondered if a dog was in the house.

When I had seen enough, I went back through the woods, got into the Land Cruiser, and drove home.

There, I called Peter Brown at Western Security Services. He was out. Rats. I left a message for him to call me. I wondered who else might be able to give me the information I wanted.

While I wondered, I made myself a sandwich out of the last of the bread in the fridge and some slabs of smoked chicken. Delish! I'd smoked the chicken out back of the shed, in the smoker I'd made out of parts from an abandoned electric stove and an old refrigerator, both of which I'd salvaged from the town dump, before the environmentalists had seized control of it and had transformed the best secondhand store on the island into a much more expensive and much less interesting place. Gone are the days of yesteryear. Alas.

A bottle of Sam Adams went well with the sandwich. When the bottle was empty and the sandwich gone, I got myself a second beer and made four loaves of white bread, using Betty Crocker's recipe from my tattered copy of her old, red cookbook. You can think of other things while you're kneading dough, and besides, whether or not I ever resolved my problems, we were going to need bread.

I considered my scouting trip behind Alexandro's house and recognized it for what it was: a step toward being predator instead of prey. I didn't feel bad about it, but I didn't feel good, either. I was facing an ancient dilemma: what to do when confronted by evil without becoming just as evil. I knew one thing: if one evil was to prevail, I wanted it to be mine.

O Socrates, O Kant, O Buber, where art thou when I need you?

I kneaded the bread and left it to rise the first time while

I made another phone call, this one to Mattie Skye, up in Weststock, Massachusetts, where, after a summer at their farm on the Vineyard, she and John and the twins were housed for the winter while John taught at the college.

"J.W. What a surprise!"

"I thought you might want to know that I've hauled *Mattie* and put her in your barn, and that I'll batten down your place in case it looks like Elmer is really going to show up."

"Thank you. I'll tell John."

"And there's something else. You're up there surrounded by intellectual types, right?"

"John might argue that, knowing the faculty and students as well as he does!" She laughed.

"I need some background information on a couple of people, and it occurred to me that some computer whiz might be able to get it for me."

"I'm afraid I'm no computer whiz, and neither is John."

"And neither am I. But you probably know somebody who is. Do you?"

"They're everywhere these days," she said. "Let me think. Hmmmm, yes, I can think of a couple. Let me grab a pencil. Now, who are the people you're interested in?"

"Three young people out in Hollywood. Two actresses: Ivy Holiday and Julia Crandel. And an offscreen cousin of Julia's named Buddy Crandel. He's with a talent agency, or some such thing."

"Ivy Holiday? Isn't she the one who dazzled the audience at the Academy Awards ceremony this past March?"

"That's Ivy, all right. But right now, all three of these people are here on the Vineyard. In fact, I just talked to them this morning. What I want to find out is everything possible about their backgrounds: where they were born, where they grew up, where they went to school, and particularly whether they were ever in any trouble, or in jail, or anything like that. I'll take anything your person can dig up."

"Why don't you just ask them, since they're right there?"

"I may do that, but I want to know what they might not tell me. That's why I need your help."

"Sounds serious. All right, I'll make some calls right now. But I warn you that you may not find out a lot, in spite of what you may have heard about the infinite information out there on the Internet."

"I'd like a rush on this, if you can manage it."

Kind Mattie was instantly concerned. "Is something wrong, J.W.? Are you in trouble of some kind?"

I put a smile in my voice. "Oh, no. My only problem is that Zee and the kids are on the mainland visiting her folks, and I'm over here sleeping alone in a double bed for a few more days. No, this business is about something else. But I do need a quick response, if I can get it."

"I'll get right on it, then. Give Zee our love when you talk with her, and keep an eye on Elmer!"

"I will."

I hadn't talked with Zee for a while, in fact, and had a sudden longing for her voice. I phoned her folks' house, over in Fall River. To my happy surprise, she answered the phone.

"We've just come back from the Whaling Museum in New Bedford," she said.

"How are the tots?"

"The tots are being spoiled rotten by their grandparents, as you might guess."

"And how are you?"

"Thinking island thoughts, more and more. And you?"

"Beginning to have erotic dreams. Hugging pillows in my sleep. Growing moody. Leering at sheep."

She laughed. "Take a lot of cold showers. We'll be home soon."

"I'll try to hold out."

"Save some of your strength for when I get there."

"I'll do my very best."

When I hung up, I was aware of time compressing.

I phoned Peter Brown again. He was still out. I told the woman who answered the phone what I wanted: all the background I could get on Ivy, Julia, and Buddy, especially problems with the law, if any. She said she'd give Brown the message. I said it was important and that I needed the information ASAP. She said she'd tell him that, too.

I punched down the bread dough, divided it, put it into four pans, and covered them with a damp dish towel.

I got another Sam Adams and went up onto the balcony. The flowers in their boxes and hangers and garden spots still looked good, but the vegetable garden was pretty thinned out. Only late-summer and fall stuff was still there. My giant pumpkin, lovingly tended all summer, had never gotten very giant at all. It looked nothing like the picture on the front of the seed package. I wondered how it would be for pies and soups and bread. Not bad, probably. Future experiments would reveal the truth.

Beyond the garden, the waters of Sengekontacket Pond were empty of the surf sailors who practiced there during the summer, and beyond the pond, only a few cars were parked along the barrier beach that was so packed between June and Labor Day. On the blue waters of the sound, beyond the beach, a lone sail, far out, was reaching toward Nantucket. The air was clear and soft, and a gentle wind moved through the trees and pushed against my hair. There was no hint of Elmer, churning northward beyond the curve of the earth, or of such people as the Vegas brothers.

Eden, where God walked in the cool of the day.

Where the serpent lurked.

I thought of all of the policemen who were zeroing in on the Vegas brothers. I figured they would keep Alberto and Alexandro pinned down for a while, but if Alberto and Alexandro were simply patient enough to outwait their watchers, sooner or later the cops would be drawn back to their regular duties, and Enterprise Management would be back in business, with Alberto providing the brains up front and with Alexandro contributing the tricks that would persuade potential customers to sign up.

In fact, Alberto didn't really have to wait for the cops to go home, since the contracts he was peddling were technically quite legal. Alexandro, being watched night and day, might not be able to burn any more houses down, or to break any more windows or windshields, or to beat anyone else half to death with a tire iron, but maybe he didn't need to. Maybe all Alberto would need to do was to remind potential customers of such past events in order to sign them up.

And the same memories would keep his current clients quiet. Having already been intimidated once, they would stay that way. Eddie Francis and his like were not about to testify against the Vegas boys in court and risk having their businesses go up in flames. Most people are not heroic, and you can't expect them to be.

My beer bottle was long empty. I went downstairs, turned on the radio, and put the bread into the oven.

Elmer had picked up speed and was coming up the coast. There was building surf and a hurricane warning from Florida to the Carolinas, and a watch as far north as New Jersey. Bermuda was battening down. There seemed to be three possible tracks for the storm: curving in toward Cape Fear, curving out to sea between Bermuda and Cape Cod, and coming straight into the south coast of New England. None of the weather forecasters was putting money down on which way the storm would go.

When the loaves were done, I sawed off a thick, steamy slice from the end of one of them, then rubbed butter on their crusts and covered them again with a slightly damp dish towel. I slathered more butter onto my slice of bread and ate it. Deelish! There is nothing better than hot, fresh bread and butter.

The next morning it was still a great combination. After breakfast, I licked my fingers, got into the Land Cruiser, and drove to Oak Bluffs.

23

Cousin Henry Bayles lived not far from the Martha's Vineyard Hospital, in a small house near Brush Pond, overlooking the Lagoon. The address in the phone book wasn't too specific, but for reasons I could not recall, I had a distant memory of the place. I guessed that my father might once have showed me the house as we passed by on our way to somewhere else, for Cousin Henry was a rather notorious character, whose home may have been noted by the curious.

The Bayleses were, of course, Betsy Crandel's people, Philadelphia folk of whom Cousin Henry was most definitely a black sheep. The socially conscious Bayleses of Philadelphia were not accustomed to having gangsters as kin, and Cousin Henry had not been given extensive coverage by the keepers of the genealogies.

His house was the opposite of the Crandel place, being small, discreet, and half-hidden from view behind trees that grew beside a street few people used. Stanley Crandel didn't mind being seen and admired, but Cousin Henry preferred anonymity. And who could blame him, since there were probably still some mobsters down in Philadelphia who were pretty mad at him.

I drove down the short, sandy driveway that led to his house, got out, and stood there long enough for anyone inside to have a look at me and decide whether I was one of those mad Pennsylvania guys.

The house was built low to the ground and had a porch running along two sides of it, one in the front and one on the side facing the Lagoon. It was neither notably neat nor notably shabby, but somewhere in between. Chairs and a table were on the porch overlooking the water, and a path led down to the beach. A small combination garage and barn was out beyond the fireplace chimney, on the far side of the house.

Beyond the barn, through some trees and undergrowth, I could see water that I took to be Brush Pond. Cousin Henry's house was on a sort of peninsula, backed on two sides by water. The only automobile entrance was the way I'd come in. I was reminded of maps I'd seen showing how early fortifications were often built inside protective river bends, so as to make it harder for attackers to come at them.

When I thought I'd stood there long enough, I went up onto the front porch and knocked on the door. It opened immediately, and I found myself looking down at a little, mahogany-skinned woman whose age could have been any-where between forty and a hundred and forty. She had small, black eyes and kinky, gray-black hair done up in a bun. She was wearing what people used to call a housedress. It was blue and the skirt seemed a bit longer than was currently fash-ionable, although who's to say what's fashionable these days? Certainly not me. She held a large dog on a leash.

"Yes?" Her voice was sharp, like a bell.

"My name is Jackson. I want to speak to Henry Bayles."

"Mr. Bayles is busy. I'm sorry." She began to shut the door.

"It's about a relative of his. Julia Crandel. Actually, it's about another relative, too. Buddy Crandel."

She studied me silently, then said, "Wait here. I'll see if he can be interrupted." She shut the door.

Seabirds called to one another as they flew above the Lagoon, and on the far side of the drawbridge, the site of the only stoplight on Martha's Vineyard, the *Islander* was heading out of Vineyard Haven toward Woods Hole. Maybe I'd be smart just to get on it and go over to America for a while, until the Vegas situation was resolved. But if I did that, maybe it wouldn't get resolved.

Vanity, vanity. The graveyards are full of absolutely essential people.

The door opened and Cousin Henry looked up at me with expressionless dark eyes in an expressionless dark face. As with the woman, it was impossible for me to judge his age, although I knew he had to be sixty or better, since he and Stanley Crandel had played together as kids. He looked, in fact, unchanged from when I'd seen him when I was a child. He was a little man, thin, as though made of wire. His hair was short and gray, and his neck was thin. He had narrow shoulders under his white shirt. He didn't look like anyone you should fear, but I knew that he was.

"Yes?" His voice was soft, like fog.

"Your cousin Julia Crandel is having a problem that I'm not sure I can solve. She's here on the island for a holiday with a friend from California. A girl named Ivy Holiday. Another cousin named Buddy Crandel just got here, too. They're all in the movie business, one way or another. The problem is a guy named Alexandro Vegas. I think he broke into the Crandel place out on East Chop, while the women were in there. I think he did this, too." I lifted my sling. "I also think he beat a young cop nearly to death, and that he's the muscle for his brother Alberto's protection racket."

I stopped talking.

"Why are you telling me this, Mr. Jackson? What's any of this have to do with me?"

"Nothing, maybe, unless you decide that it does."

"I care nothing for Buddy Crandel. I didn't like him as a child, and I have no feelings for him at all now that he's grown-up. I also care nothing about the fate of young policemen or about local hoodlums and their criminal activities."

"That leaves Julia. Maybe you care about her. And for what it's worth, the young cop who's in the hospital got between Alexandro and her in front of the Crandel place. I think Alexandro caught up with him later because of that."

"You think a lot of things, Mr. Jackson, but you don't seem to have much proof of anything."

I looked down at him. "That's right. Sorry to have interrupted your work. Good-bye."

I turned away and was going down the porch stairs when he said, "Wait."

I paused and looked back at him. He gestured to the porch chairs that overlooked the Lagoon. "Sit down there. Excuse me for a moment."

He went inside and I sat down. It was a nice view. An outboard motorboat was tied to a small dock at the foot of the path leading from Cousin Henry's house to the beach. It looked like the sort of boat a man used to go fishing. Far up the Lagoon I could see Alberto Vegas's boathouse and dock.

Cousin Henry came out of the house carrying two glasses of iced tea. He gave one to me and sat in the other chair. "You can begin by telling me about yourself, and how you got involved in this matter. Then tell me the rest."

I told him about my work for the Crandels and about the faucet and everything that had occurred on the island since Julia and Ivy had arrived.

He didn't say a word until I was through. Then he said, "You're leaving things out. You haven't talked about the killings in California."

"I don't think they have anything to do with what's happening here. Alexandro Vegas is the local problem."

"Tell me about the rest of it."

I did that, telling him everything I knew. When I was through, he said, "Now I know what you know. Tell me what you think."

"I think that Alexandro is a dangerous sociopath with a special hatred for blacks, although he's got plenty of hate to go around to everybody else. I don't know if he was born bad or whether his childhood and his prison experience made him that way, but whether it's nature or nurture, Alexandro is as bad as I've seen. I think he's a bomb, and that the only thing that's keeping him from exploding is his brother, Alberto, who's even more dangerous than Alexandro because he's smart. The cops can't do anything about either one of them, because all they've got are suspicions, so if Alexandro does blow up, they won't get him till afterwards, which might be too late for Julia and Ivy."

"What about the two bodyguards? They're professionals and they're armed."

I sipped my tea. It was good. "If you wanted to rape and kill Julia Crandel and Ivy Holiday, do you think two professional armed guards could stop you?"

He didn't look at me and he didn't answer.

I said, "Of course there's Buddy Crandel, too. He makes three men, all told."

"Buddy Crandel was a crybaby as a child. I doubt if he's changed. I imagine he'll run if he gets the chance."

So much for Buddy Crandel as defender of the weak.

"Where are Stanley and Betsy?" asked Cousin Henry.

"Switzerland, I think. I don't know where, exactly."

"Stanley has a lot of money and could probably take care of this problem if he was home."

"Maybe I can find out where he is."

Cousin Henry emptied his glass and put it on the table between us. "On the other hand, Stanley and Betsy probably shouldn't get involved. Their reputations are important to them, after all. No, I think it's probably best to let them enjoy their travels." He looked out at the Lagoon. "In fact, Mr. Jackson, I think it might be best if none of us get involved."

I tried to take that in. Then I said, "I'm afraid some of us are already involved, Mr. Bayles." I finished my drink, put my glass beside his, and got to my feet. "Well, I'll be going. Thanks for the tea."

"Thank you for coming by."

I glanced at him and thought I saw a fleeting, ironic smile before that ebony face again became expressionless.

"These things sometimes resolve themselves," he said to my back as I walked to the Land Cruiser. "We should never despair."

He was standing on the porch, a tea glass in each hand, as I drove away.

I turned on the radio and listened to the classical music station over on the Cape. They were playing opera selections, and I recognized Pavarotti's voice. He was singing "Una furtiva lagrima," and it was enough to break your heart.

As I drove along County Road, the station gave a weather report. Elmer had picked up speed and was churning along at a good clip. Hurricane watches now reached as far north as Massachusetts, and it seemed that the three tracks that Elmer might take had been reduced to two: one that led straight on into the south coast of New England and one that curved out to sea south of Cape Cod. Coastal evacuations were being advised, even though the storm was still at least two days away.

Whichever track the storm took, the Vineyard should prepare for high winds and seas. I was glad that I'd hauled the *Mattie* and the *Shirley J.*, but now I had some more work to do. In light of Elmer's prospective arrival, Alexandro Vegas became a secondary concern. Such is often the case when natural disasters occur: seemingly important problems become unimportant; people who ordinarily won't speak to each other combine forces to help each other out. As has often been observed, nothing unites people like a common enemy. Big Brother was smart to have Oceania fighting constant wars.

I drove home and began to batten things down in expectation of a major league blow. That I was pretty much working one-handed made ordinarily simple tasks more complex. Taking the flower boxes off the fence and putting them on ground was a problem, as was taking the chairs and table off the balcony and putting them and all of the lawn furniture away in the corral behind the house, where I kept stuff too big to store in my shed. Taking down the hanging flower baskets and bird feeders was easier. I wished it were as easy to put the Vegas brothers out of my life.

But if wishes were dollars, we'd all be rich.

24

The place was about as ready as it was going to get, and I was resting my aching bones and muscles and having a pre-supper snack of Sam Adams accompanied by smoked blue-fish pâté on crackers when the phone rang. It was Mattie Skye.

"I have a hacker here, J.W. Is that the right word? Anyway, would you like to talk to her?"

Hackers, or whatever the word was, came in both genders, apparently. "Put her on."

"Her name's Darlene. Here she is."

"Hi," said Darlene. "I may have something for you."

"Great."

"Ivy Holiday was easiest because she's the best known of the three people you're interested in, and she has a fan club on the Net. I think I have more material than you might want, in fact."

"What interests me most is whether she or the others have had any personal problems or problems with the law: arrests, fights, accusations, anything like that. And I'd like to know the other people involved, if any."

"Yes, Mattie said that sort of thing interested you. Well, in Ivy Holiday's case, there's quite a trail, because she's got a temper. Did you see her at the Academy Awards?"

"No, but I read about it."

"Well, that's classic Ivy. Here's some of what I got: She was born and raised in Texas. She and her father didn't get along, and she got married when she was sixteen to a drummer in a band. That's where she got the name Holiday. She was Ivy Washington before that. The marriage lasted about a year and ended in flames. It was a pretty rough one, I guess. Anyway, she went one way, he went the other. I don't know who beat up the other one the most before they split, and I don't know what happened to him. He just dropped out of sight.

"She moved to California to be an actress and married a guy named Montgomery, but kept the name Holiday. He was another actor wanna-be. Only a few months later, he was killed in an accident. A combination of booze and drugs, apparently. He fell down the stairs in their apartment building and broke his neck."

"Ivy has hard luck with husbands."

"Some people do. They'd both been living pretty fast and loose in L.A. with a crowd of people a lot like them. Anyway, a few months after he died, Ivy was nailed, along with some others, for using coke at a party. Nothing much came of it.

"About that time her career improved even though she lost a couple of roles because she'd gotten pretty militant about racial stereotypes and the way women were treated in the industry. The scene at the Academy Awards was part of that. She's marched in parades and protested against sexism and racism, and got arrested once for a scuffle at a sit-in. She doesn't back down from anybody if she thinks she's right or thinks somebody's trying to take advantage of her, or of blacks or of women, or especially of black women.

"The most serious thing she's been involved with was a stalker named Mackenzie Reed. Do you know about him?"

"I do. And I know about Jane Freed and Dick Hawkins, too. Unless you know something about any of that business that I don't know."

She told me what she knew, and it was even less than I knew.

"That's about it for Ivy, then," said Darlene. "Shall I keep looking? Do you need more?"

I wanted to know everything, of course, but I said, "That'll do for now. Thanks. What about the others?"

"Thinner pickings, although I do have some stuff about both of them. There's more about Julia Crandel, so I'll start with her.

"She went to Brown, which seems to be a family tradition, and then went to New York to be an actress. She dated in Providence, but didn't have a real romance until she got to New York. She lived for several months with a guy named Sam Pierson, who was working on Wall Street. They broke up and she lived alone for a while, then shared an apartment with girlfriends. She got busted with some friends for smoking pot—can you believe that people still get busted for that?—then had another boyfriend for a while, a guy named Flynt. About that time she began to get roles on and off Broadway. After a year or so, they broke up, and she decided to try her luck in Hollywood."

"That marijuana bust was the only problem she had? Were the breakups with the boyfriends rough?"

"Some hurt feelings, maybe, but only that. They met, they lived together, they went their separate ways. Very civilized."

"Modern romance."

"You got it. Anyway, she went out to Hollywood and has been there ever since, trying to get her foot in the door, and keeping her head screwed on pretty well while she's doing it. The only time she and the law ever met was at a New Year's party that got out of hand. She and some others spent the night in jail, and it cost them a little money to get back out on the street. My impression is that she was pretty embarrassed about the whole thing."

"What about her relations with Jane Freed, the psychiatrist who was killed?"

"Yeah. I noticed that Julia and Ivy had the same therapist. A lot of people have psychiatrists, though."

"But Freed was killed."

"Not by Julia Crandel or Ivy Holiday, apparently."

Apparently.

"Tell me about Buddy Crandel," I said.

"Not too much on Buddy, I'm afraid. Most of what I got, I got from a friend out in L.A. who has friends who know people like Ivy and Julia and Buddy. Anyway, Buddy's originally from Hartford and did the Crandel-family thing by going to Brown, then moved to California to get into the movie business. I guess he decided pretty fast that he wasn't movie-actor material, so he worked at other jobs before he got on with the agency he's working for now. He doesn't have any criminal record as far as I could find out, but he does have the reputation of using women in what people used to call a pretty cavalier manner, even by Hollywood standards. I guess he's a good-looking guy, and women fall for him pretty easily. He charms them, then he dumps them. My information is that he's left some pretty angry women in his wake, but there's no law against that, so his record is officially clean. Sounds like a real scumbag, to me."

It was the first sign of female resentment that Darlene had revealed. A lot of women are pretty mad about guys like Buddy Crandel, I guessed. And who could blame them?

"You might like him if you met him," I said, just to be perverse. "He's a good-looking, sweet-talking guy."

"Save me from such people!"

"Stay up there in Weststock and you'll be safe. Thanks a lot for your help."

"What's going on, anyway? Mattie says you used to be a policeman. Why do you want to know about all this stuff?"

"I'm just nosy. Thanks again. Can I call for you again, if I need more information?"

"Only if you tell me what it's for."

"Deal."

I rang off and was surprised to note that the sun had set. It had been a long day. My arm and leg hurt. I ate supper, took some aspirin, hoped that the cops were keeping a sharp eye on Alexandro, locked the doors just in case they weren't, and went to bed.

In the morning, I woke to that odd yellow-sky calm that sometimes precedes a hurricane. There was no wind; there was a strange, almost eerie look to things, and an ethereal quality to the light and the feeling of the air. I wondered, as I had before, if perhaps it had something to do with high, invisible clouds or winds that changed the effect of the sun's rays. Whatever the cause, the famous calm before the storm was not just the stuff of folklore; it was really happening once again.

I listened to the news. Elmer was coming straight at New England and picking up speed. I swallowed a couple more aspirins with my orange juice, then had coffee with a full-bloat breakfast: bacon, fried eggs, English muffins slathered with butter and this year's homemade bluebarb jam. It was full of cholesterol and calories, but delish and just what I'd need to start me on a day of hurricane preparations at John Skye's farm and some other places I took care of during the winter.

I washed the dishes, stacked them in the rack, and was headed out of the house when the phone rang. It was Lisa Goldman with some news I didn't like.

"Our guy dozed off in the wee hours and Alexandro's loose. You'd think a guy that big would be easy to find, but we haven't found him yet. He's probably in his own Caddie, but we don't know for sure because he might have bullied somebody into loaning him a car. Keep your eyes open. I think he's mad at you."

Terrific. And I'd been sleeping hard while Alexandro was out there on the prowl. I was glad I'd locked the doors, even though the locks wouldn't have done much to slow Alexandro down if he'd decided to come in. Or, for that matter, any more than they'd stop anybody else who really wanted to get in, since my house was not a fortress and locks are only deterrents to honest people.

I don't like locks, and I refuse to be one of those people who on principle lock everything, always. But this time, when I left the house, I locked it behind me even though I knew full well the gesture was as meaningless as a rose in bloom or wind in dry grass.

Alexandro the arsonist didn't even need to break in; he only needed a can of gasoline to turn my house to ashes.

I drove first to John Skye's farm and made sure everything was buttoned down: shutters fastened, doors secure, blowable stuff stashed in the barn. I was conscious of limping, and my bad arm hurt, but I kept at my work until it was done. Then I went on to the next house and worked there for another hour. It's remarkable how much stuff has to be tended to when a big blow is coming: flowerpots, lawn furniture, screens and screen doors, boats, cars, and anything that might be picked up and thrown through a window or into the middle of next week.

I went from house to house all morning, working at such chores, then, satisfied that I had done what I could do, I drove down to Edgartown through the preternatural yellow air, passing houses where people were doing the same things that I had been doing.

On Main Street, merchants were taking in anything they still displayed on the sidewalks and were taping windows or nailing plywood over them.

At Collins Beach, men were hauling boats and trailering them away, working fast but steadily with a minimum of wasted energy. The harbor was already emptier than it had been when I'd hauled my own boats and would be emptier still by tomorrow, when Elmer was scheduled to arrive, if he didn't go out to sea first.

Out on the glassy water, I could see Roger Goldman putting triple lines on the *Kayla*. Farther out, the *Invictus* hung on her mooring, her bowline limp and sagging. If she were my boat, I'd be putting more lines on her or maybe moving her someplace where she was less likely to be struck by another boat broken free from her mooring and blowing downwind across the harbor. Many a securely tied boat has been wrecked in that way.

But *Invictus* wasn't my boat, and nobody seemed to need my help, so I circled back and parked in the lot at the foot of Main.

Mike Smith's truck was parked in front of the yacht club, which meant that he was busy squaring things away inside or up at the club's tennis courts. The club's boats were already out of the water, I noted. Mike, being a careful, well-organized guy, had probably started hauling them as soon as Elmer seemed to be considering coming to New England. There was a good chance that tomorrow the water would be over the floor of the club and, in fact, over the lot where I was now parked, so Mike had his work cut out for him.

I went into the Dock Street Coffee Shop. The regulars were lined up along the counter, and the talk was about Elmer, the effect he would have on the upcoming Derby, and an occasional aside about the Red Sox, who, it being September, were far out of the race, now that Clemens was gone. You have to be hardy or stupid or eternally optimistic or all three to be a Red Sox fan, but I am one of them.

"What happened to you, J.W.?" asked the waitress, putting a cup of coffee in front of me.

"I'm just wearing this sling so I'll get the sympathy I think I deserve for living the wretched bachelor's life while Zee's over on the mainland visiting her folks."

"Poor baby. But you'd better tell her to stay there till this storm goes by. It looks like we may get it on the nose. After lunch, we're closing up and packing things above the high-water mark until things quiet down. What'll you have?"

I had a burger and hash browns and more coffee.

Around me, voices spoke of hurricanes past, compared experiences, and speculated about Elmer with that combination of fascination and fear that characterizes talk of natural disasters. When I went outside again, the air seemed yellower and the mirrored water more ominous.

I had a sense of doom, a primeval feeling that forces beyond my ken were taking control of my world. I didn't like it.

— 25 —

Where was Alexandro? Hiding out until dark, until he could wreak havoc upon some enemy? Me, for instance? Or was he even on the island? Maybe Alberto had sent him to America, and he was hunkering down someplace over there until the cops all had to return to their regular shifts, and it was time for him to come home again and go back to work as a terrorist.

Or maybe he'd decided to just drop dead out of sheer orneriness.

Sure.

I was tired and sore. I drove to my driveway entrance and turned in. I stopped the Land Cruiser and looked down the sandy drive. Had another car come in since I'd left? Was its driver waiting for me down at the house, or in the trees?

I remembered the pistol under the seat and took it out and put it beside me. Then I drove down to the house.

No one was there.

I walked around to the shed and the corral, pistol in hand.

Nothing. No sign that anyone had been there.

I unlocked the front door and went through the house.

Nobody.

I was clearly becoming as paranoid as those people who lock their houses all the time. Not good, kemo sabe.

I stuck the pistol in a pocket and phoned Zee.

"We're coming home," she said immediately. "I don't

want you to be over there alone when Elmer comes. We're catching an afternoon boat."

The very last thing I wanted.

"No," I said in my firmest voice. "You and the kids stay there. It'll be a lot safer."

"We're coming."

"No. Your folks' place is a lot sturdier than ours. I want you all over there."

But Zee was not one to take orders. From me or anyone else.

"I'll call you when we get to Vineyard Haven, Jefferson. It's no problem getting from here to the island; the only problem is getting from the island to the mainland. According to the news, the Vineyard standby line is already out of sight, and there are already some fights."

That was no doubt true. Tourists caught on islands when big storms are brewing have sudden, strong desires to be on bigger hunks of land, and they can get testy when they discover that ferryboats can carry only so many cars and can make only so many runs a day, no matter what disaster seems pending.

But I knew Zee, so I was ready for her argument. I also knew I didn't want her and our children over here with both Alexandro and Elmer on the prowl. The thought gave me chills. There are times in life that call for lies. This seemed to be one of them.

"No," I said. "Listen, sweets, I called to tell you I've screwed everything here down as tight as I can, and I've got reservations on the last boat tonight to Woods Hole. Do you understand? I got them through the chief. He's a cop. He's got pull. I'm bringing the cats, and I'll drive to your folks' place from there. I should get to Fall River in the small hours. I want all of us to be together tomorrow if Elmer actually does come this way. That's what I've been trying to tell you. I don't want you coming here, because I'm going there!"

"You're coming over here?" A note of doubt was in her

voice, and no wonder. No other storm had ever sent me to the mainland.

"It's just a fluke," I said. "I was talking to the chief, and he just happened to have this ticket. One of his people was going over to Barnstable on some kind of business, but the meeting was canceled because of the storm, so I took the ticket. I decided I'd rather have all of us there than all of us here."

"Well . . ."

"Tell your mom to expect an extra mouth for breakfast. And buy some cat food." I thought the reference to Oliver Underfoot and Velcro gave a nice credibility to my story.

"She'll be happy to see you. So will Dad." In spite of the cat reference, Zee was hearing something in my voice that I didn't want her to hear. Wives are like that, and most of the time I think it's fine. This time I didn't.

"I love you," I said, using an ancient ploy of distraction. "Kiss the kids for me, and tell them the cats and I will see them in the morning. I'll see you earlier. We can lock your bedroom door, can't we?"

We'd been apart for days, and there was no real reason for her to think I was lying. So she laid aside her intuitions.

"I love you, too," she said. "I'll be waiting for you to get here! I miss you in my bed!"

"Me, too."

Betrayed by love, she rang off. I hung up and put my head in my hands. Zee did not take to being protected. I just hoped that all of tomorrow's ferry runs would be canceled. Otherwise, when I didn't show up in the wee hours, and she phoned and found me home, she would be on the first boat to the island, a child under each arm, fire in her eyes, me in her sights.

Zee, the black panther.

Me, the lying father of her cubs.

But I'd meet that problem when it came. Meanwhile, all I had to worry about was myself.

I turned on our little TV set, which had come to the house as part of Zee's dowry. The Weather Channel was sharply focused on Elmer, who was definitely headed our way at a goodly clip, with winds well over a hundred miles an hour. Hurricane watches had been abandoned along the southern Atlantic Coast and had been replaced by warnings to the north, with New England now the odds-on-favorite spot for the winds to hit the mainland. I checked a couple of Boston channels, and they, too, were full of news about the storm and advice to coastal communities to evacuate low-lying areas.

The ancient hunting camp that my father and I had slowly transformed over the years into a year-round house was built low to the ground and had weathered nearly a century of storms. Although it was old and drafty, I had no reason to think that this hurricane would do it in any more than past hurricanes had done. The winds might uproot our gardens and knock down some of our trees, or even rip off some shingles from the roof and blow out some windows, but the next day, when the skies were blue again, the house would still be standing, and looking not unlike it had looked before. I was glad, though, that we weren't nearer the water, for storm tides are dangerous. When great winds work the great waters, great destruction can ensue.

But Alexandro could wreak great destruction regardless of how far my house and I were from the water, and no one knew where he was. While I considered these facts, the phone rang and things got even worse.

It was Lisa Goldman. "J.W? Do you happen to know where that Mills guy and Ivy Holiday are?"

I felt a little chill. "No. Where are they supposed to be?"

"We just got a call from Julia Crandel. Ivy Holiday and Mills took Mills's car to go down to South Beach and see if the surf was up yet, and they haven't come back. They were supposed to be home for lunch. Julia and Mills's partner are worried."

I said the first word that came to mind. "Alexandro?"

"Hell, I don't know. They haven't even been gone long enough for us to put out an official missing-person's bulletin, and it may be nothing at all. Probably they drove to Gay Head or something and just didn't bother to phone in. But things being what they are, I'm putting out a call for people to be on the lookout for them."

"Have you checked Alexandro's house?"

"Nobody home. Even that woman of his is gone. And I've got no good excuse for a search warrant."

"How about Alberto's place?"

"Ditto. He and his wife are at his office, putting plywood on the windows. Besides, this doesn't smell like Alberto's work. He may beat up his wife and girlfriends, but kidnapping isn't his game. Too dangerous. He's smart. He wants to be rich and live long."

I thought of Alexandro's hatred and lust. It wouldn't be too dangerous for him. And he wasn't smart.

"I've got people looking, and I've called the other island police, but everybody's pretty busy getting ready for the storm," said Lisa. "There may be nothing to this, but keep your eyes open. I don't like the way it feels."

I didn't either.

I got my lockpicks and drove to Oak Bluffs. How many times had I made that trip in the last week? A thousand?

I drove to the development where Alexandro lived. There, beside the road leading to his house, was the same parked car that had been there before. The West Tisbury cop inside had finished his newspaper and was reading a paperback novel. I parked in front of him and walked back. He looked at me and I looked at him. After a bit of this, he rolled down his window.

I told him who I was and who he was and asked him how Lisa Goldman knew that Alexandro had disappeared.

"How should I know?" he asked, not sure what I had to do with things. I told him, and then he was friendlier. "Oh, yeah. I hear Vegas gave you that arm. Well, he came home last night and parked that big black Caddy of his in the driveway. The guy who was here ran out of coffee about midnight and nodded off about two. When he woke up an hour later, Vegas's car was gone, and nobody's seen it or him since."

"Maybe he's in the house. Anybody go in and find out?"

"We got no search warrant and no way to get one since nobody's got anything on him." He sounded disgusted.

"Anybody knock on the door?"

"Yeah. Me. Nobody home. The dame who lives there with him pulled out at dawn. The guy who followed her says she went home to her folks up in Chilmark. Like I said, the place is empty now, but I'm going to sit here and watch it anyway, in case I'm wrong or in case somebody comes back from wherever they are."

I guessed that the woman didn't want to be alone when the storm hit, and I recalled the saying that "home is the place where, when you have to go there, they have to take you in."

The cop looked tired. I thought he was mad at whoever had dozed off.

"I'm going to bang on the door," I said. "If Alexandro's hiding in there, I'd like to know it."

"Go to it. But if he is in there, he may decide to break your other arm."

I drove to the house and knocked on the door. The cop had been right; the place did have that empty feeling about it. I knocked hard a couple more times. Nothing.

I drove away, waving at the cop as I passed. I took a left onto County Road, another left onto Barnes Road, and another onto the road that led toward the back of Alexandro's house. I parked again behind the empty summer house where I'd parked before and went through the woods until I came to Alexandro's backyard.

It was still cluttered and unkempt. I watched the windows for a while, then crossed the yard and banged on the back door.

Silence.

I tried the knob. Locked. I took out my picks and was inside in less than a minute. I was getting better at picking, and the lock was an easy one. Why did people put such cheap locks on even expensive houses?

I stood with my back to the door and listened. I heard nothing but the ticking of a clock.

I was in a mudroom behind the kitchen. It was dirty and cluttered with boots and stray gear. In one corner was a five-gallon can half-filled with gasoline. I went into the kitchen. Dirty dishes were on the counters and the sour smell of old food filled the air. I went through the whole house, careful not to touch anything. No one was there.

I decided to do some more looking.

There was no sign that the house's inhabitants had much knowledge of brooms or other cleaning materials or were inclined to put things away once they'd used them. Maybe the Vegases were related to the Snopes and the Beans.

But I was soon glad that Alexandro and his woman were slobs, because twenty minutes after I started poking around, I found what I'd hoped to find, amid the other rubbish in a basement workroom: some remnants of canvas, a role of waxed twine, and some nylon strapping. Alexandro wasn't smart enough or neat enough to get rid of the materials he'd used to make the bags he'd slapped over Larry Curtis's head and then over mine. It might not be evidence that would hold up in court, but it was enough for me to know for sure that Alexandro was responsible for my broken arm and the attack on Larry Curtis.

I went upstairs and out into the mudroom. There I paused and looked at the can of gasoline. I even put out a hand toward it. But then I went on out the back door the way I'd come in, wiped away any fingerprints I might have left on the doorknob, and walked back to my car.

After Joshua had been born, Zee and I, as nervous, new, amateur parents, had bought ourselves a cellular phone that we carried around in whichever car was away from home. We almost never used it, but somehow it made us feel good to have it, especially when we and the tots were out on the distant beaches of Chappy, far from Dr. Spock and other folk who knew more about babies than we did. No crisis had ever induced us to use the phone to call our pediatrician, but one never knew, so the phone was always with us.

And it was with me now.

I phoned the Crandel house. Harley answered immediately. I identified myself and said, "I hear that your partner and Ivy went off to watch the waves. Are they back yet?"

"No."

"When did they leave the house?"

"Three hours ago. They should have been back by now."

"Did you see them leave?"

"Yeah."

"Did you see a black Caddie about the same time?"

After a short silence, he said, "Yeah. It came from up the street. What—?"

But I'd hung up.

I phoned Alberto's house. An answering machine replied. I left no message, but instead called the offices of Enterprise Management Corporation. This time I got a human being, such as she was: Sylvia Vegas. I told her who I was and said that I wanted to talk to Alberto.

She called me a seven-letter word. I said again that I wanted to talk to Alberto. Better yet, that I wanted to see him.

"Well, you better hope that he don't see you. You do and he's liable to reach down your throat, grab you by the balls, and turn you inside out!"

I thought it possible that he could actually do that. "I want to talk with him."

"Well, that's too damned bad. He don't want to talk to you! He's working."

My voice felt hot. "You tell Alberto that his little brother has probably kidnapped two people, and that they're all missing. Tell him that! And tell him he'd better start working with the cops before Alexandro kills somebody!"

"Go fuck yourself," she shouted. But she hesitated a moment before slamming the phone down.

As I drove toward Edgartown, the sleeping wind was beginning to wake and stir the trees. I turned on the radio and heard the latest about Elmer. He was hurrying north, picking up speed.

26

The parking lots for Al's Package Store and the A & P were jammed with cars, as their drivers stripped the shelves of booze, food, water, batteries, candles, Sterno fuel, and whatever else they thought they might need if the electricity went off for a few days. Such raids on stores always occurred before big storms. I doubted, for instance, if any portable generators were still for sale on the island. If so, their sellers were no doubt getting good prices. It's a rare disaster that's bad for everybody; someone usually profits by it. Liquor stores do well whatever happens: if the news is good, their customers buy to celebrate; if it's bad, they buy to mourn. Because of this, some folks believe that a liquor store is the most perfect of businesses.

I went down Cooke Street, took a right onto Peases Point Way, and drove south to Katama. Already, a lot of cars were parked near the beach, as people checked out the rising surf. Such storm surfs are popular entertainment for coastal dwellers, and it's not at all unusual for swimmers to cavort in the waves or, occasionally, for some fun-seeking person to be drowned in them.

I eased along, looking for the car in which I'd first seen Mills and Jack Harley when they were parked in front of the Crandel house. I never found it, but in the parking lot at the Herring Creek end of the public beach, I found a large black Cadillac. Other cars were in the lot, as well, and people were walking to and from the beach, laughing and

talking the way they do when they know a big wind is coming but it hasn't affected them yet.

I peeked inside the Caddie and saw food containers, cigarette butts, and beer cans—the kind of mess that I'd come
to expect from Alexandro. But no people were there. The
doors were unlocked. Who would dare steal Alexandro
Vegas's car, after all? I walked toward the surf on the far side
of the dunes. The water was gray and the waves weren't too
big yet, but swells were rolling in from the south, reaching
far ahead of the winds that had created them. The sky was
pale blue, made wan by high, thin clouds. Toward the horizon the clouds were thicker and darker.

Several dozen people, mostly on the youngish side, were
on the beach, playing tag with the waves or just watching
the white water of the surf. A few young men were out in
the water, laughing and shouting. I had done that sort of
thing myself at one time; but not now. I studied the crowd,
but didn't see Alexandro, Mills, or Ivy Holiday. I walked
among the people, asking them if anyone had seen them. I
soon learned that Ivy's name was usually enough identification, and that I didn't need to give a description of her. But
no one had seen her or anyone who looked like either of the
men. I worked my way west, toward the distant haze that
was Squibnocket, through a thinning crowd, asking everyone I met. Finally, well away from the area where most of
the surf watchers had gathered, I got a possible ID.

A young man and woman seated on a blanket beside a
break through the dunes that led from the beach to the
parking lot had seen a girl who might have been Ivy, but
she wasn't with a man who looked like Mills; she was with
the biggest man either of them had ever seen. The girl had
apparently been sick, because the man was helping her,
almost carrying her, out to the parking lot. They had come
from that way, over toward the west.

I got a feeling I didn't like and walked west. After a while,
far ahead, I could see something awash in the surf, and I

began to run. Mills's body, still clothed, was rolling and slipping, first toward shore, then toward the sea. I got to him and with my good arm dragged him up away from the grasping waves. He was heavy, and his clothing was weighty with water. When I got him up onto dry sand, I yelled down the beach, but I knew the sound of the sea would prevent anyone from hearing me. I put a finger to Mills's throat and an ear to his chest. Nothing. I rolled him over and worked on him. Water came out of his mouth. I worked on him more, then shouted down the beach again, and then worked some more, knowing all the time that I was doing no good. It was too late for Mills; he had gone to some other place and wasn't coming back.

After a while I gave up and trotted back to the east. I paused at the blanket to ask the young couple to keep an eye on the body, then went to the Land Cruiser and phoned the police.

The sirens brought two cruisers and an ambulance, and a bit later, a rush of curious surf watchers, anxious to see what catastrophe warranted such interest by the authorities.

The young couple closest to the disaster quickly became experts whose opinions were greatly in demand.

I told Tony D'Agostine how I'd come to find the body. Tony had heard the missing-person story, but like most cops in prestorm time had been too busy to do much looking on his own. I showed him the Caddy. He took a look around the parking lot.

"The big guy and the girl must have taken off in Mills's car. Maybe somebody saw them go. You describe the car?"

I told him what it looked like and said he should call Jack Harley for particulars.

Tony nodded. "Mills here has a holster on his belt, but no piece."

"I noticed that. Maybe it's in the surf."

"Maybe. Alexandro is a convicted felon, so he can't own a piece of his own. Not legally anyway."

"Maybe he doesn't have to buy one, now."

"Yeah." Tony got on the cruiser radio for a few minutes, then went out to the entrance to the parking lot to stop anyone who might have seen something from leaving. Soon more sirens came from Edgartown, and the parking lot became fairly well populated with cops, including members of the sheriff's department and Olive Otero of the state police.

Olive gave me a sour look. One of the reasons we don't get along is because she thinks fishing is a waste of time. How can you like someone like that?

"You," she said. "I should have known. Jackson is just another word for trouble."

"Now, Olive," I said. "No snobbery, please. Just remember that I'm the public and you're my servant."

She snarled and started up toward the beach as the deputies and the Edgartown cops gathered around Tony, then scattered to question everyone on hand as to what they had or hadn't seen.

I phoned the emergency ward at the hospital. No, no one resembling Ivy Holiday had come in. So much for wishful thinking. I hung up and phoned the Crandel house. Jack Harley answered in a professionally neutral voice. I told him what I'd been told and had seen on the beach. He swore.

"You be very careful," I said. "Don't let Julia out of your sight!"

"Yes." His voice was shaky, but calm. "I'll call Boston and get some more help down here right away. Jesus. Poor Willy."

Willy. So Mills had a first name, too. I'd found out a little late.

I went over to Tony and told him about my calls. "I can't tell you any more about the situation here," I said. "I'll come by the office later and give you a statement. Meanwhile, I'm going on the assumption that Alexandro has the girl. He's just fool enough to do something like this and think he can get away with it. Somebody had better find him and do it fast. The guy's finally killed somebody!"

Tony nodded. "Yeah. I've called the chief and told him the same thing, and he's going to get on it. This is an island, so Alexandro can't just drive off of it. He's still here somewhere. We'll find him."

"The quicker, the better. Maybe Alberto knows where he's gone."

"Alberto Vegas hates cops!"

"Alberto loves Alberto, though. Maybe you can make a trade: Alexandro for taking some heat off of Alberto's business transactions."

Tony grunted. "It ain't up to me to make any deals like that, but I'll send the idea along."

"If the chief doesn't like that notion, maybe he'll like the one that Alberto loves Alexandro so much that he's hiding him and Ivy Holiday someplace. In his own house, maybe. Has anybody looked there?"

"Don't ask me. Ask the OBPD!"

I did that on my car phone before I left the parking lot, first telling Lisa Goldman about the body on the beach and what the young couple had reported to me. Lisa told me that since we'd last spoken she had persuaded Alberto that it was in his best interest to prove that Alexandro wasn't in Alberto's house and had been given a fast tour of the place to prove it.

"He wasn't happy about showing us his house, but he did it," said Lisa. "Then I put an officer on watch to make sure Alexandro didn't slip in after we left. We're going to have to look for him and the woman someplace else."

Where? "Did Alberto have any idea where little brother might be?"

"I asked him that, and he said he didn't."

Honest Alberto.

I didn't think we had much time to find Ivy. My best hope

for her, in fact, was that Alexandro would want to do a lot of things to her before he killed her. For that, he'd need privacy.

Privacy.

I drove to Edgartown and parked in the lot at the foot of Main. People were still taping glass, fastening shutters, taking down swinging signs, and nailing plywood over windows. Over at Collins Beach men were still hauling boats. A wind was blowing.

Near the dock where Alberto had moored the Whaler, I found the car belonging to Mills and Harley. The Whaler and *Invictus* were gone.

I walked over to the harbormaster's shack on the town dock and stuck my head inside. The harbormaster was out, as might be expected what with Elmer on his way. Like the cops, he had enough to do under normal conditions; with a hurricane coming, he had even more. But one of his young assistants, Carl Duarte, was in the shack, talking into a radio. When he was through, he looked at me and I asked him who had gone aboard the *Invictus*. He shook his head.

"I don't know. She headed outside an hour or two ago, is all I can tell you. There's been a lot of coming and going on the water. People bringing in their boats, and whatnot."

"I'd like to know who went aboard her."

"I'll ask the boss. I don't think he's been home since yesterday morning, what with helping guys, and all."

Duarte turned and spoke into his radio. The harbormaster's voice crackled back. "That's the Vegas boat. No, I don't know who's aboard her. I been busy down-harbor quite a while and wouldn't have seen anybody coming or going. Maybe you can raise her on the radio."

"Will do." Duarte put aside the speaker and rubbed his chin. "You want to contact the boat, J.W.?"

What could I lose? "Sure. Give it a try. Find out who's on board and where they're going."

Duarte made his call, but got no answer. He tried several times, then looked at me and shrugged.

I looked out at the harbor, where the wind was now stirring the once flat waters.

"It's beginning to breeze up," said Duarte.

It was beginning to breeze up in my psyche, too. I walked back to the Land Cruiser and drove over to the Reading Room dock, where I found a parking place amid other trucks. Maybe somebody there had seen something.

On Collins Beach, most of the dinghies normally tied alongside the dock were gone. The ones remaining had been carried up to the back of the beach and made fast to the fence there. With luck, the tides wouldn't get that high. Frank Goulart was hauling his ten-footer to his truck, so I gave him a hand loading it. He wiped his brow.

"You're getting old, Frank," I said. "Come a storm warning, you're usually the first one out of here, not the last."

"Yeah. Gettin' slow, I guess."

"You see anybody go aboard the *Invictus*?"

"Yeah. In that Whaler. Guy was sober, but the girl looked drunk. Couldn't even stand up. Wouldn't want a drunk woman on a boat of mine. Not with this blow coming. Damned fools, if you ask me."

But I was already turning away and heading for my truck.

27

If Lisa Goldman said that no one was in Alberto's house,
then no one was in Alberto's house. But she hadn't said anything about the *Invictus*. Maybe because she didn't know the
boat was there. After all, the dock was below the bluff and
maybe out of sight of the house, and the last thing Lisa had
heard about the boat was that she was on a mooring in
Edgartown. Or maybe she'd gotten there after Lisa had
searched the house. Or maybe the boat wasn't there at all. If
she wasn't, where was she?

Through the rising wind and falling darkness, I drove
along Barnes Road till I came to Alberto's driveway, where,
as Lisa had said there would be, I saw a parked car with a
police officer in it. Leaves and a few small branches were
beginning to blow from the trees as I stopped, rolled down
my window, and said, above the sound of the wind, "I'm
J. W. Jackson. Is Alberto at home?"

"I know who you are," she said. "I've seen you in the station. No, Alberto's back at his office. Nobody's here."

A car was parked beside the house, at the head of the
road leading down to the dock. I pointed at it.

"That's his wife's car," she said. "But she's with him at the
office. I'm telling you that there's nobody in the house."

"I think I'll go knock on the door."

"No. It's probably better if you don't. The place isn't
actually a crime scene, but it'll be better for everyone if you
don't go down there. You should leave this business to the
police."

"Are you going to arrest me if I go down there?"

"Look, I know you want to help, but you'll really be help-ing if you just go home and stay there until this is over."

"Do you know if the *Invictus* is down at the dock?" As I spoke, I heard a low rumble. It sounded like distant, rolling thunder, and it came from beyond Alberto's house.

"The *Invictus*. That's Alberto's boat, isn't it? Well, as far as I know, the *Invictus* is in Edgartown."

The wind sang through the trees, and the thunder rolled. I raised my voice. "She's not down there anymore. Alexandro took her out today and he had Ivy Holiday with him."

"What!" She reached for her radio. "I'd better report that! Stay right there."

But in that moment I knew what the thunder was.

"You hear those engines?" I shouted. "That's the *Invictus*! She's headed out of here!"

I slammed the Land Cruiser into gear and spun gravel as I sped down the driveway. Sylvia Vegas's car blocked the road that led down to the boathouse and dock, so I skidded to a stop beside the house, jumped out of the truck, and ran, limping, past the car and down the road.

The *Invictus* was moving away from the pier, with a giant figure at the controls on the flying bridge. I ran out on the dock as the boat cleared the last piling and made a wild leap just as Alexandro pushed his throttles forward and the rumble of the engines became a roar.

I didn't reach the cockpit, but I did reach the boarding platform on the stern, where I landed with a crash that sent a searing pain through my left arm and nearly as bad a one through my injured leg. I almost went overboard as the boat surged forward, but got a grip on a cleat just in time and pulled myself up against the transom. I hung there, below the cockpit railing, as the boat picked up speed.

If Alexandro had seen me, he gave no sign of it as he drove the boat out toward the drawbridge. Where was he going? Over to the mainland to escape island law? Maybe, but not likely.

I remembered what Lisa Goldman had told me: that Alexandro thought black women who think they're God's gifts to the world should be screwed until they know their places, then kicked off the steamer dock with rocks tied to their necks. Too many people were around the steamer dock for him to do that, but there weren't any witnesses on the *Invictus*. Alexandro was going out into the sound to rid himself of Ivy Holiday.

I wondered if Ivy was dead or alive. He'd brought her to this dock where he could make his boat fast and devote all of his attention to her. Now he was through with her, and I didn't want to think of what he might have done.

I groped for my pistol and realized it was gone. Somewhere, maybe on that gimping run from the Land Cruiser to the dock, we'd become separated. Damn. I had never wanted or needed a weapon more.

I looked back at the pier and saw the police officer scrambling back up the road toward the house. While she was calling people, I hoped she'd call the Coast Guard.

I got onto my knees and peeked over the transom. Alexandro had eyes only for what was in front of him, which was wise, considering the rising waves and east wind into which he was heading. The *Invictus* was powerful and heavy, though, and split the water cleanly as she drove up the Lagoon. But if the waves were rising in this sheltered place, I knew they must be worse out in the sound, even though the full force of the hurricane was still hours away.

Offering prayers to broken stone, I slipped over the transom into the cockpit of the boat and, eyes on Alexandro, scuttled forward until I got to the hatch leading to the lounge beneath the flying bridge. Then, still unseen, I slipped below, shutting the hatch behind me.

The lounge was luxurious, with generous seating, a bar, a carpeted deck, and windows on every side. Stairs led down to cabins both aft and forward. The aft cabin was, I guessed, the master bedroom. I took a deep breath and went down the ladder, past the engine room, fearing what I would find in the captain's cabin.

I found nothing. I looked in the private head and in the many lockers and under the queen-size bed. But there was no sign that Ivy had been there. Alexandro apparently wasn't about to intrude upon Alberto's private quarters.

I felt a change in the motion of the boat and heard a different sound from the engines. I went back up into the lounge and looked out a window. We had passed under the drawbridge and were now in the entrance to Vineyard Haven harbor, between East and West Chop, churning northeast, taking the white-capped waves on our starboard bow. *Invictus* was beginning to pitch and roll and throw spray to her lee, but she put her shoulders to the sea and moved steadily ahead. I hoped that Alexandro was not as stupid about handling a boat as he was about other things, because if he was, this storm could bring us all to grief.

I took the forward ladder and found myself in a combination galley and dining area. A storage cabin and a head, complete with shower, were to starboard, and a narrow bunk room was to port. Crew quarters, probably, should Alberto ever want a crew. Forward was a door leading to what, in this boat, was surely a sleeping cabin. I went to the door and opened it.

Ivy Holiday, bloody and motionless, lay naked on the double bed, crucified, her arms spread and tied to the bedposts. No part of her was unbruised, unbeaten. The lovely bones of her face looked broken beneath the swelling flesh that covered them. Her sleek skin was a mass of welts and blood. Her wrists were raw beneath their bonds, and her fingers looked as though they had been broken one by one. Blood was between her legs, and on the bedclothes beneath her.

I went to her and touched her throat. She moaned and I

saw that her perfect teeth were now only bloody gums. She was alive, but barely. I was filled with fear and rage.

Two worthless emotions. I pushed them away. I wanted to be cold, not hot.

I got out my pocketknife and cut away Ivy's bonds. I wrapped her in the bloodstained bedspread. I tentatively tried to pick her up, but when I did, my bad arm was shot with fire. I laid her back down.

I looked around the cabin. A hatch was in the ceiling, leading out onto the foredeck. Stored under the bed I found the ladder that could be attached to the deck beneath the hatch and would allow people to pass between deck and cabin without going aft. I wrestled it into place, then went out to the storage room and got a length of line and two life jackets. I got one jacket on Ivy and strapped it tight and put the other aside for myself.

Returning to the galley, I found a meat cleaver and several knives. I took the cleaver and the sharpest of the knives, then went to the storage room to see what else I might find in the way of weapons. The swordfishing harpoon was there, and I took that. And I found an ax. I put the harpoon and the ax in the cabin with Ivy and peeked up into the lounge. Alexandro was still up on the flying bridge.

I went up into the lounge and looked out at the water. Night was coming fast. The sea was gray-black, and every wave had whitecaps being blown to leeward. The *Invictus* was off West Chop, heading across toward Cape Cod, with the waves banging against her starboard bow and sending water and foam flying across her deck. She was pounding, but she was strong. I wondered how far out Alexandro planned to go before he came below to tie some weight to Ivy's neck and toss her overboard. I looked back at West Chop. The lighthouse was almost directly downwind of us, and my memory of the tides told me that they were falling to the west.

I didn't have much time. I got the ax and went to the engine room. With the ax I cut the fuel lines. I was back in the forward cabin when the great engines sputtered and died.

Immediately the living thing that the *Invictus* had been became a dead creature, tossed and rolling in the rising waves. In moments Alexandro would be coming below to see what was the matter. I shut and locked the door behind me, then climbed the ladder, opened the hatch an inch, and looked up at the flying bridge. Alexandro was gone. I threw open the hatch. The roar of the wind and sea filled my ears, and water sloshed over the foredeck and poured into the cabin, drenching me.

I tied the line around Ivy and laid her over my left shoulder. My bad arm screamed at me. I went up the swaying ladder and with what seemed the last of my strength, thrust her out onto the tossing deck and lashed her to the hatch. Then I went back down and put on the other awkward life jacket.

As I was tying the last tie, I heard Alexandro screaming invectives. He'd been to the engine room and seen the cut fuel lines and now he was searching the boat. It wouldn't take him long to reach the forward cabin. I picked up the ax and began hacking at the hull of the boat with my good arm. It was a strong hull, made of thick fiberglass, but the ax was sharp and adrenaline filled my veins. The ax went through and I cut again and again as water spurted up at me. I chopped and chopped again, and more water came, and then I saw the door shake as Alexandro put a shoulder to it, howling curses.

The door wouldn't stand against him for long, I knew. I put down the ax and took up the harpoon and threw it. The razor-sharp barb went through the wood and I heard a sharp cry from the other side.

I couldn't tell if it was a cry of pain or surprise or both, but I didn't wait to find out. I went up the ladder and out onto the deck. I loosed the line from the hatch and tied it around my waist. Then I got Ivy's body under my good arm and went overboard with her.

28

The water was wild but not too cold. September water, not winter water. Still, we couldn't stay in it too long before hypothermia would begin having an effect on us. When the waves lifted me, the line linking me to Ivy would tug at me and the wind would hit me, but I would be able to see the glimmer of the West Chop light. Then I'd sink into a trough and again the line would tug, but now I could see nothing.

Somewhere behind us, upwind, the *Invictus* was taking on a lot of water. I wondered briefly if Alexandro had been hit by the harpoon, and if he could swim. Then I put him out of my mind and concentrated on my own swimming, one armed, downwind through the gathering darkness toward West Chop.

I swam and swam, then rested, exhausted, and let the waves carry me whither they would. I pulled Ivy close to me and tried to tell if she was still alive. But she was wet and cold and I couldn't be sure. Then I swam some more, wondering if the light was getting closer or whether the wind and tide were going to carry me past the point of land and on down Vineyard Sound until, at last, the cold grip of the sea would carry my warm life away and leave my corpse floating, floating, lashed to Ivy's. Would I of coral be made? Would I suffer a sea change into something rich and strange?

I rested, then swam, then rested, then swam. My legs were iron, my arm was becoming lead. My eyes were full of salt, my skin was cold. The light seemed no nearer.

I swam and swam and knew I wasn't going to reach the shore. I hoped Zee wouldn't be too unhappy. I hoped my children would live good lives and not suffer because they had no father. I wanted to tell them that we all have a death to die and that no one should be too sad when it happens.

But I didn't want to die. I wanted to see Joshua and Diana and, most of all, Zee. I swam.

And then surf was all around me, with towering, crashing waves and roiling sands, and I was being swept up onto a beach, then carried out, then swept up again. I dug my fingers into the sand and clawed my way forward. A wave carried Ivy up beside me, and I grabbed her life jacket before the next ebbing wave jerked her back into the thundering black surf. A wave crashed down on my back and my face was full of sand and water. I choked and gagged and the surge of water carried me and Ivy high up onto the beach. I got to my knees and was knocked down. I gasped for air and tried to stand. My legs were like water and collapsed under me. I had no strength. I got up onto my knees; I took hold of Ivy's life jacket with my swimming hand; I backed up the beach. The surf clutched at us, but I went backward until I could go no farther and fell onto the wet sand.

The wind was howling now, and my teeth were chattering, but we were out of the water. Beside me, Ivy lay still as death. I was too weak to carry her. I looked around, trying to see through the darkness. Some sort of shrub was growing there. I tried to untie the line from my waist, but the knot was too much for me. I dug into my pocket and found my knife and got it open with my teeth and cut the line. I rested, then dragged Ivy to the bush and tied her to it so she couldn't wash away if the water rose too high before I could get back.

I rested some more, until I was afraid that if I stayed longer, I would perish from the cold. Then I willed myself up onto my feet and started inland to find help.

Fortunately, I didn't have far to go, for some West Chop

folk were out looking at the stormy sound. I gave them
quite a shock as I staggered into their view, but they were
quick to respond. Some went running down to the beach
and others picked me up and carried me to a nearby house
where they gave me tea and phoned for an ambulance.

I rode to the hospital in Oak Bluffs under a siren and was
greeted at the emergency ward by faces I knew pretty well,
since most of them had worked there with Zee for years.
They asked me questions, examined me, got me into bed,
and gave me something that put me to sleep, but not before
I told them to call Zee and tell her I was fine.

As I drifted away, I asked about Ivy and was told that
she'd been flown to Boston by helicopter just before the real
winds began to blow.

When the big winds finally slowed down, I had visitors:
Julia Crandel and Jack Harley, both grieving; Lisa Goldman, to tell me that the *Invictus* had drifted down onto the
rocks off West Chop and had broken up on them, and that
Alexandro was missing, presumed drowned.

They didn't let me get out of bed until Hurricane Elmer
was only a fading low-pressure system somewhere off to the
east of Nova Scotia. Thus, I missed his visit and would have
no tales to tell of his mighty winds and high tides, no brag-
ging rights.

I was giving the nurses such a hard time by the time
Elmer was gone that it was clear to everyone that I should
be thrown out of the hospital. Lisa Goldman came by and
picked me up and took me to get my truck, which was
parked by the police station, having been driven there by a
cop who had picked it up in Alberto Vegas's driveway.

"And there's this," said Lisa, handing me my old .38.
"Our gal Peggy found it on Alberto's dock after she ran
down there trying to keep you from being an idiot. You
should be more careful with your hardware."

"I will be."

"First boat from Woods Hole will be over in an hour. I

understand that your family is aboard. You might want to meet them."

"Wise advice, Officer."

And I took it.

And after Zee and I were through being lovey and Zee was over the first stages of being furious, we drove home and found a lot of branches down, some screens blown out, and two cats who acted as if nothing had happened, but pointed out that their food dishes were getting pretty low and reminded us that they hadn't had their afternoon snacks for a while.

It was a fine day, as is often the case when a storm has just passed, and we worked all afternoon cleaning things up and getting straightened away. Then we fed the tots and played with them in the living room, then put them to bed.

We sat on the couch and I told Zee everything that had happened. When I was through, she shook her head. "I'm never going to be able to leave you home alone again, Jefferson!"

It seemed impolitic to tell her that I was glad she and the kids hadn't been here, since they'd have been just three more things for me to have worried about.

"Yes, dear," I said. "You're absolutely right."

"Don't 'yes, dear' me, Jefferson. You're just saying that so I won't know that you're glad the kids and I weren't here because we'd just have been three more things for you to worry about!"

Smart Zee. I pulled her closer with my good arm. "Yes, dear. You're absolutely right."

"I'll whack your bad arm if you don't stop that!"

I nuzzled her. "Yes, dear."

"You're hopeless!" She turned toward me. "Oh, am I glad to be back!"

"Me, too. And I'm glad this business is all over." My lips looked for hers and found them. Kisses sweeter than wine.

Bachelors are fools.

But as it turned out, the business wasn't quite over.

Pete Warner's wife didn't survive her heart attack. A week after they buried her, Pete, wearing a long coat, drove to Alberto Vegas's house and knocked on the door. When Alberto opened it, Pete emptied two barrels of buckshot into him, then drove to the police station and handed the gun to the kid at the desk.

A week after that, Ben Krane's office burned down. Arson. No clues.

Zee and I discussed the fire while we fished on East Beach. "Ben was the only one left for Cousin Henry to get at," I said to her as I reeled in. My left arm still hurt, but you can't let a little hurt keep you from fishing. "Ben never did anything to the Crandels, but he was tied to the Vegas boys, and I guess that was enough for Henry. It's sort of like the Lord smiting evildoers unto the umpteenth generation."

"Yeah. Or a plague on all their houses. Of course, Henry might not have had anything to do with it. A lot of people hate Ben Krane. How do you think a jury will handle Pete Warner?"

"With kid gloves."

"I think so, too. Hey! Did you see that swirl!" She flipped her rod just a bit to make the lure jump. "There he is again. Hit it, fish!"

The fish tried but missed.

"Drat," said Zee. "I don't think Henry would have done anything about it if what happened to Ivy had happened out in L.A., but it happened in OB, where he lives. Remind me never to make Cousin Henry mad at me."

"No one could possibly be mad at you, sweets," I said. "Well, blast and drat! Will you look at that! He takes a swipe at my plug and he hits yours!"

Her rod was bent and the fish was a good one.

"That's my fish!" I shook my fist at the sky. "I'm married to a fish thief!"

"No one could possibly be mad at me, sweets," said Zee,

showing me her snow-white grin. "Just reel in so you don't tangle my line, and then go up and tend to the kiddies while their mom is busy doing woman's work."

I did that and watched her land the biggest blue of the day and the third biggest in the whole Derby as things turned out. But we didn't know that then.

One thing we did know was that *Island of Emeralds,* starring Zeolinda Jackson and some other actors and actresses, would have its East Coast premiere on the island just before Christmas. Zee and I and other locals who had helped out when the film had been made were invited, along with various bigwigs and other island denizens deemed worthy of the honor.

Zee could hardly wait. When we'd gotten the news, she'd beamed at her son. "Will I be the face on the cutting-room floor? Or will I be a shining star? Afterwards, will I still speak to a mere mortal such as your dad? What do you think, Joshua?"

"Stay tuned," I'd said to Diana, feeding her a sip of beer.

The best thing that happened was that Larry Curtis surprised everyone by coming out of his coma with only short-term memory loss. He had no recollection of being beaten and was past the worst of his healing pains before he even knew he needed fixing.

"It'll take a while, but we expect him to be back on the job before too long," said Lisa Goldman.

Ivy Holiday was not so lucky. She never woke up and died two weeks after they airlifted her to Boston. Hollywood mourned; her friends mourned; even I mourned, but it didn't keep me from phoning William Peterson Calhoun and telling him what I thought.

"I can't prove anything, of course," I said. "But you might be able to dig up enough to get your man another trial. Get in touch with a PI out there named Peter Brown. He knows a good deal about the case, and he may be able to help you out."

Calhoun was careful. After all, he couldn't be sure I wasn't just setting his client up for a fall. "You think that if we dig into Ivy Holiday's past, we'll find a pattern of violence."

"She was a hothead. She was passionate. She didn't like to be crossed. She did irrational things. That bare-breasted stunt, for instance. Her first husband hasn't been seen since they broke up. Her second one fell downstairs and killed himself. Her roommate, who started dating the guy who left Ivy, gets stabbed a dozen times. By your client, they say, but maybe not, because that many cuts strikes me as an act of passion, and he had no passion for the roommate. Ivy's shrink, the woman she talks to, confesses to, maybe, gets knocked off by somebody who didn't break into the office. Her fatherly old landlord, who likes to put his hands on the ladies who rent his apartments, gets run over by a car. I think there's a pattern there, but maybe you don't. It doesn't make any difference to me. Ivy's dead, and I don't plan on selling my story to the *National Planet*."

"What about the letters? Somebody sent them to her."

"Not your client, according to you. Check out Ivy's printer or typewriter or whatever she used to write."

"But why would she keep writing them to herself?"

"You're the hotshot lawyer. You figure it out. Maybe she wanted to keep people thinking that your boy Mackenzie Reed was still after her, so they wouldn't have any second thoughts about him being guilty. Or maybe a shrink can explain it. I know one thing: Julia Crandel always seemed more nervous about the letter writer than Ivy did."

Calhoun was still thinking about all that when I hung up.

In December, *Island of Emeralds* appeared on the screen of the new theater in Edgartown. The islanders who saw it spent most of their time noticing how a character would walk out of a house in Vineyard Haven and immediately be in a yard in Edgartown; how the hero would get in his car and drive a long distance to the house next door; how cute all the local children were; and how nice the island looked.

Kevin Turner and Kate Ballinger, the nominal stars of the film, were on hand and were interviewed by the *Gazette* and the *Times* and by the mainland papers, whose columnists were glad to have an excuse to go down to the Vineyard all expenses paid. The stars were quoted as saying how beautiful the island was and what fine folks the islanders were.

Zeolinda Jackson's face did not land on the cutting-room floor. During her minute or so on the screen, she spoke her one line and owned the camera. No wonder the *Boston Globe* interviewed her. No wonder she dazzled the reporter. No wonder the film's producer predicted that if she wanted a career in Hollywood, she could probably have it.

The wonder was that she didn't.

"I'm too busy right here," she said to the *Globe* reporter. "I'm a nurse, I have two little kids, and I have a husband who gets into trouble whenever I'm gone."

The reporter turned to me. "And what do you say to your wife about that, Mr. Jackson?"

I had Joshua on one knee and Diana on the other. I bounced them a bit and smiled at their mom. "I say, 'Yes, dear. You're absolutely right.' "

RECIPES

CHRIS'S BEAN DIP

2 cans of kidney beans, drained and rinsed
⅓ medium onion, chopped fine
1 garlic clove, minced
⅓ cup mayonnaise
⅓ cup relish
dash of dry mustard
salt and pepper

Mix all ingredients together and refrigerate several hours. Serve with tortilla chips.

J.W. stole this recipe as he has stolen others and now considers it his own. It is, of course, delish!

BLUEBARB JAM

1½ cup rhubarb (about 1 lb., fresh)
¼ cup water
4 cups blueberries, mashed
6½ cups sugar
½ tsp. butter
½ bottle (3 oz.) Certo

Slice thinly (or chop) rhubarb (do not peel). Simmer in ¼ cup water, covered, until soft (1–2 minutes). Crush blueberries and combine with rhubarb. Measure 3½ cups combined fruit into a large saucepan and add sugar. Add ½ tsp. butter. Mix well.

Place over high heat, bring to a rolling boil, and boil hard for 1 minute, stirring constantly. Remove from heat and immediately stir in Certo. Skim off foam with a metal spoon. Stir and skim for five minutes to cool slightly and to prevent fruit from floating. Ladle into hot jars and seal.

Makes about eight 8-oz. jars of jam.

J.W. has this as part of his breakfast in this book. He loves it, and rightly so!

RAISIN BRAN MUFFINS

IN A LARGE BOWL COMBINE:
5 cups sifted flour
2 tsp. salt
5 tsp. baking soda
2 tsp. cinnamon
2¾ cups sugar

ADD:
1 15-oz. package Kellogg's Raisin Bran cereal

MIX WELL WITH:
1 qt. buttermilk or yogurt
4 beaten eggs
1 cup cooking oil

ADD:

grated rind of 3 oranges (3 tbsp.)
1 cup chopped nuts

Refrigerate in container with tight lid. Keeps up to 6 weeks. Whenever you want fresh muffins, you bake as many as you need.

To bake: put dough in greased muffin tins, sprinkle with cinnamon and sugar, bake at 375 degrees for 20 minutes.

J.W. mixes up a batch of this wonderful dough in this book. He considers the baked product to be the world's best bran muffins. And they are!

—PHIL CRAIG

ABOUT THE AUTHOR

Philip R. Craig grew up on a small cattle ranch southeast of Durango, Colorado. He earned his MFA at the University of Iowa Writers' Workshop and is a professor of literature at Wheelock College in Boston. He and his wife live in Hamilton, Massachusetts, and spend their summers on Martha's Vineyard.